The Bridge Series

LUCKY JIM

by

KINGSLEY AMIS

EDITED AND ABRIDGED
BY D. K. SWAN

Illustrated by William Burnard

LONGMAN

LONGMAN GROUP LIMITED
London

*Associated companies, branches and representatives
throughout the world*

© Longman Group Ltd (formerly
Longmans, Green & Co Ltd) 1963

*First published in this series
by arrangement with Victor Gollancz Ltd 1963
New impressions *January, *October 1965;
*January 1967; *June 1968;
*August 1969; *March 1970;
*June 1971; *January 1972*

ISBN 0 582 53020 2

*Printed in Hong Kong by
Peninsula Press Ltd*

THE BRIDGE SERIES

THE *Bridge Series* offers interesting reading matter for the students of English as a second or foreign language who have reached a stage between the graded supplementary reader and full English. Having enjoyed a number of books in the *Simplified English Series*, such a student is ready for something more challenging.

The books in the *Bridge Series* are moderately simplified in vocabulary and often slightly reduced in length. Nearly all retain the syntax of the original writers. This has the dual advantage of giving practice in understanding more advanced sentence patterns and making it possible to keep the original flavour of the book.

Of intermediate difficulty between the *Simplified English Series* and the unrestricted English of literature, the *Bridge Series* books contain little of vocabulary or idiom that is not immediately valuable to the fairly advanced learner, and we hope that they will prove thoroughly enjoyable to read and study for their own sakes.

TECHNICAL NOTE

The vocabulary of the *Simplified English Series* is the 2,000 words of the *General Service List* (*Interim Report on Vocabulary Selection*) and there is a degree of structure control. In the *Bridge Series* words outside the commonest 7,000 (in Thorndike and Lorge: *A Teacher's Handbook of 30,000 Words*, Columbia University, 1944) have usually been replaced by commoner and more generally useful words. Words used which are outside the first 3,000 of the list are explained in a glossary and are so distributed throughout the book that they do not occur at a greater density than 25 per running 1,000 words.

THE BRIDGE SERIES

GENERAL EDITOR: J. A. BRIGHT, B.A.

INTRODUCTION

KINGSLEY AMIS, the author of *Lucky Jim*, was born in
the south of London in 1922. His first interest in literature
was in the field of poetry. At the age of eleven he was writing verse, at the university he was one of the editors of
Oxford Poetry 1949, and his own poetry has been published
in two books: *A Frame of Mind* and *A Case of Samples*.
His name is often to be seen in British newspapers and
magazines as the writer of articles and reviews.

Lucky Jim, published in 1954, was Amis's first novel. It
was something so different, so fresh and so brilliantly
clever that the critics welcomed it with excitement.

Kingsley Amis is a university lecturer[1] in English. In
Lucky Jim he takes us into a world he knows well; it is set
in a university college 'somewhere in England', but you
need not have seen a British university to enjoy this book.

I suppose you could call *Lucky Jim* an adventure story.
There is a love interest, so in a way it is a love story. In
fact, in some ways this book is like other novels we have
read. It is very, very funny—but other writers have made
us laugh. It gives us a remarkably good picture of a certain
section of society—but it is not just a social novel. In what
way is it different from the novels which were written
before it?

Let us ask ourselves another question. What used we to
expect when we read a novel? We expected to identify ourselves with one of the characters; that is to say, to live
through the happenings of the story—adventure, travel,

[1] See Glossary.

love, mystery, sorrow, happiness—with the hero or the heroine, or at least with the person supposed to be telling the story. In our imagination we *were* that person. And the hero or heroine was braver, or more noble, or in some way better than most of us are in real life.

In *Lucky Jim* we identify ourselves with Dixon, but he can hardly be called a hero—if there were such a word, we might call him an 'un-hero'. He knows he is not brave or noble, or even very good—and we know that he is very much like most of us. He is certainly real.

CHAPTER 1

DIXON had found his professor in the College Library and they were now moving across a small lawn towards the front of the main building of the College. They looked, but only looked, like some kind of funny stage act: Welch tall and weedy, with limp whitening hair, Dixon rather short, fair and round-faced, with an unusual breadth of shoulder that had never been matched by any special physical strength or skill. In spite of this over-evident contrast between them, Dixon realised that their progress, steady and by appearance thoughtful, must seem rather donnish to passing students. He and Welch might well be talking about history, and in the way history might be talked about on Oxford and Cambridge college lawns.

In fact Welch was talking rather childishly about music. How had he become Professor of History, even at a place like this? By published work? No. By extra good teaching? No underlined. Then how? As usual Dixon left this question aside, telling himself that what mattered was that this man had decisive power over his future, at least until the next four or five weeks were passed. Until then he must try to make Welch like him, and one way of doing this was, he supposed, to be present and conscious while Welch talked about music. But did Welch notice who else was there while he talked, and if he noticed did he remember, and if he remembered would it affect such thoughts as he had already? Then suddenly, with no warning, the second of Dixon's two worries snapped into consciousness. Fighting desperately against a yawn of nervousness, he asked in his flat northern voice: 'How's Margaret these days?'

The other's face showed a very gradual change of expression as his attention began to swing round to this new situation, and in a moment or two he was able to say: 'Margaret?'

'Yes; I've not seen her for a week or two.' Or three, Dixon added uneasily to himself.

'Oh. She's recovering very quickly, I think, all things considered. She took a very hard knock, of course, over that Catchpole fellow. It's her mind that's suffering now, you see, not her body; physically she's absolutely fit again, I should say. In fact, the sooner she can get back to some sort of work the better. It would help to take her mind off . . . off . . .'

Dixon knew all this, and very much better than Welch could hope to, but he felt obliged to say: 'Yes, I see. I think living with you, Professor, and Mrs. Welch, must have helped her a lot.'

'Yes, I think there must be something about the atmosphere of the place, you know, that has some sort of healing effect.' And the healing atmosphere led him back once more to the subject of music.

Dixon considered how, without causing Welch to turn on him a long-lived puzzled frown, he could remind him of his invitation to come to tea at the Welches' house outside the city. They'd arranged to leave at four o'clock in Welch's car, and it was now ten past. Dixon felt nervousness hitting out at his stomach as he thought of seeing Margaret, whom he was to take out that evening for the first time since she'd broken down. He forced his attention away on to Welch's habits as a car-driver, and began trying to feed his anger to cover his nervousness. It worked for five seconds or less.

How would she behave when they were alone together?
Would she be gay, pretending she'd forgotten, or had never
noticed, the length of time since he last saw her, gaining
height before she dipped to the attack? Or would she be
silent and dull, apparently quite inattentive, forcing him
to drag painfully from small-talk through expression of
anxiety to defeat in humble promises and excuses? However it began, it would go on in the same way: with one of
those questions which could be neither answered nor
avoided, with some frightening confession, some state-
ment about herself which, whether 'said for effect' or not,
got its effect just the same. He'd been drawn into the
Margaret business by a combination of virtues he hadn't
known he possessed: politeness, friendly interest, a good-
natured willingness to be taken advantage of, a desire for
simple friendship. It had seemed natural for a female
lecturer to invite a junior, though older, newcomer to the
staff to coffee, and no more than polite to accept. Then
suddenly he'd become the man who was 'going round'
with Margaret, and somehow competing with this Catchpole, a background figure of varying importance. He'd
thought a couple of months earlier that Catchpole was
progressing nicely, taking the strain off him. And then
Catchpole had thrown her over and left Dixon to receive
alone the full attack of those terrible questions and
confessions.

Those questions. . . . Although he wasn't allowed to
smoke another cigarette until five o'clock, Dixon lit one
now as he remembered the earliest of them, six months or
more ago; about the beginning of last December it had
been, seven or eight weeks after he took up his appoint-
ment. 'Do you like coming to see me?' was the first he
could remember, and it had been easy as well as truthful

to answer 'Yes'. Then there'd been ones like 'Do you think we get along well together?' and 'Am I the only girl you know in this place?' and once, when he'd asked her out for the third evening running, 'Are we going to go on seeing so much of each other?' His first fears had attacked him then, but before that and for some time after he'd thought how much simpler this kind of honesty made the awful business of dealing with women. And the same had seemed true of the confessions: 'I do enjoy being with you', 'I don't get along well with men as a rule', 'Don't laugh at me if I say I think the Board did a better job than they knew when they appointed you'. He hadn't wanted to laugh then, nor did he want to now. What would she be wearing this evening? He thought he would just be able to praise anything except the green Paisley dress in combination with the low-heeled velvet shoes.

Where was Welch? Dixon found him in one of the passages.

'Thought you'd gone without me, Professor,' he said.

The other turned, his face twisted with wonder. 'Gone?' he asked. 'You're . . .'

'You're taking me home for tea,' Dixon informed him. 'We arranged it on Monday, at coffee-time, in the Common Room.'

'Coffee-time?'

'Yes, on Monday,' Dixon answered him, putting his hands into his pockets and tightening them as fists.

'Oh,' Welch said. 'Oh. Did we say this afternoon?'

'That's right, Professor. Hope it's still convenient.'

Welch was recovering quickly. He managed to put his fishing-hat on his head. 'We'll go down in my car,' he offered.

'That'll be nice.'

Outside the building they walked to the car where it stood with a few others. Dixon stared around him while Welch looked thoroughly for his keys.

A minute later he was sitting listening to a sound like the ringing of a cracked door-bell as Welch pulled at the starter. This died away into a high-pitched humming that seemed to involve every part of the car. Welch tried again; this time the effect was of beer-bottles being struck unevenly. Before Dixon could do more than close his eyes he was pressed firmly back against the seat, and with a tearing sound from underneath the wheels the car burst forward towards the grass, which Welch ran over briefly before turning into the road.

They climbed College Road, keeping to the middle of the highway. The despairing horn of a lorry behind them made Dixon take a secret look at Welch, whose face, he saw with passion, held an expression of calm assurance like an old seaman's in rough weather. Dixon shut his eyes again. He was hoping that when Welch had reached the top of the hill the conversation would turn in some other direction than History Department matters. He even thought he'd rather hear some more about music or about Welch's sons, the unmanly writing Michel and the bearded pacifist painting Bertrand whom Margaret had described to him. But whatever the subject for discussion might be, Dixon knew that before the journey ended he'd find his face becoming shapeless, like an old bag, with the strain of making it smile and show interest and speak its few permitted words, of steering it between breaking down in utter weariness and tightening with murderous rage.

At last Welch said in a far-away half-shout, 'Oh, by the way, Dixon.'

'Yes, Professor?'

'I've been wondering if you'd care to come over next week-end for the . . . week-end. I think it should be quite good fun. We're having a few people from London, you know, friends of ours and of my son Bertrand's. Bertrand's going to try and come himself, of course, but he doesn't know yet if he can get away. I expect we shall put on one or two little shows, little bits of music and so on. We'll probably ask you to join in something.'

The car was running along a clear road. 'Thank you very much, I should love to come,' Dixon said, thinking he must get Margaret to do some spying to find out what he'd probably be asked to join in.

Welch seemed quite glad at this ready acceptance. 'That's fine,' he said, apparently with feeling. 'Now there's a Department matter I'd like to discuss with you. I've been talking to the Principal about the College Open Week at the end of term. He wants the History Department to contribute something, you see, and I've been wondering about you. I thought you might like to give the evening lecture the Department is to provide, if you could.'

'Well, I would rather like to have a go at a public lecture, if you think I'm capable of it,' Dixon managed to say.

'I thought something like "Merrie England" might do as a subject. Not too donnish, and not too . . . not too . . . Do you think you could prepare something of that sort?'

CHAPTER 2

'And then, just before I became unconscious, I suddenly stopped caring. I'd been desperately holding on to the empty bottle, I remember, as if I were holding on to life, in a way. But quite soon I didn't in the least mind going: I felt too tired somehow. And yet if someone had shaken me and said, "Come on, you're not going, you're coming back," I really believe I should have started trying to make the effort, trying to get back. But nobody did and so I just thought, Oh well, here we go, it doesn't matter so very much. A curious sensation.' Margaret Peel, small, thin, wearing glasses and bright make-up, glanced at Dixon with a half-smile. Around them was the low noise of half a dozen conversations.

'It's a good sign that you're able to talk about it like this,' he said. She made no reply, so he went on: 'What happened afterwards, or can't you remember? Don't tell me if you'd rather not, of course.'

She pulled her cardigan up over the shoulders of the green Paisley dress and told him.

There was a last question which Dixon knew he was compelled to ask. He said in a low voice, having first drunk freely from his glass: 'You needn't say anything if you don't want to, but . . . you are over this business, aren't you? You wouldn't think of trying again, I mean?'

She glanced up quickly as if she'd been expecting to be asked this, but he couldn't be sure whether she was glad or sorry when it came. Then she turned her head away and he could see how thin the flesh was over her jawbone. 'No, I wouldn't try again,' she said. 'I don't care about him any more; I don't feel anything at all about him. In

7

fact I feel now it was rather silly to have tried at all.'

This made Dixon decide that his fears about this evening had been foolish. 'Good,' he said cheerfully. 'Has he tried to get in touch with you or anything?'

'Nothing, not even so much as a telephone message. Vanished without a trace. He might never have existed—as far as we are concerned. I suppose he's too busy with his popsy these days, as he said he'd be.'

'Oh, he said that, did he?'

'Oh yes, our Mr Catchpole never made any secret about things. What were his words? "I'm taking her away to North Wales with me for a couple of weeks. I thought I ought to tell you before I went off." Oh, he was charmingly frank about it, James; quite charming in every way.'

Again she turned away from him, and this time he found himself noticing the thinness of her neck. He felt for his cigarettes, but before he could offer them to her, she turned back with a little smile which he recognised, with self-dislike, as consciously brave.

She emptied her glass with a quick gay movement. 'Beer,' she said. 'Bring me beer. The night is young.'

While he was getting the drinks, Dixon wondered first how many more he might be expected to pay for, and then why Margaret, with her full lecturer's salary uninterrupted by her absence from work, so seldom offered to buy him a drink. Finally, though this was no more welcome, he thought of the morning before Margaret had taken a whole bottleful of sleeping-pills. He'd had nothing to do at College that day before a lecture in the afternoon, and she'd been free after seeing some students at ten. After coffee at sevenpence a cup in a recently-opened restaurant, they'd gone to a chemist's where she'd wanted to buy a few things. One of the things had been a new bottle of the sleeping-pills. He could remember exactly how she'd looked dropping the bottle, in its white paper wrapping, into her handbag and glancing up to say: 'If you've nothing better to do tonight I'll be making tea about ten. What about dropping in for an hour?' He'd said he would, meaning to go, but he hadn't been able to get his next day's lecture written up in time, nor, he realised, had the prospect of another conference about Catchpole seemed inviting when ten o'clock came. In the early evening Catchpole had called on Margaret to tell her that he was finished with her, and at about ten she'd taken the whole bottleful of pills. If he'd been there himself, Dixon thought now for the thousandth time, he'd have been able to prevent her, or, if too late for that, to get her to the hospital a good hour and a half earlier.

'By the way, James,' Margaret said, taking her glass, 'I want to say how grateful I am to you for your understanding during the last couple of weeks. It has been good of you.'

Dixon made himself ready for anything. Puzzle remarks that sounded harmless or even pleasant were the surest sign of a coming attack—the mysterious horseman riding towards the gold-carrying coach. 'I didn't know I'd been so understanding as that,' he said in an uncoloured tone.

'Oh, just the way you've been keeping in the background. You were the only one who took the trouble to think it out, that I might prefer not to be showered with kind inquiries, "and how are you feeling, my dear, after your unpleasant experience" and so on. Do you know, old Mother Welch had people from the village who'd never even heard of me before, dropping in to ask how I was. You know, James, they couldn't have been kinder, but I'll be very glad indeed to get out of that place.'

It seemed genuine. She had sometimes in the past taken some of his laziest or most hurtful actions or inactions in this way, though not, of course, as often as she'd taken as lazy or hurtful some action intended to help. Perhaps he could now begin to head the talk somewhere else.

'How much longer are you thinking of staying with the Neddies?'

'Oh, not more than a couple of weeks, I hope. I want to get out before the summer vacation in any case. It all depends on how soon I can find somewhere to live.'

'That's good,' Dixon said, his spirits rising as opportunity for greater honesty seemed to be approaching. 'You'll be there next week-end, then.'

'What, for Neddy's arty get-together? Yes, of course. Why, you don't mean you're coming, do you?'

'Yes, that's just what I do mean. The question was put to me on the way down in the car. Why, what's so funny?'

Margaret was laughing in the way Dixon had named to himself 'the tinkle of tiny silver bells'. He sometimes thought that the whole of her behaviour came from translating such phrases into action, but before he could feel much annoyance with himself or her, she said: 'You know what your week-end will be, do you?'

'Well, fine talk mostly, I hoped. I can talk away with anybody. What's the plan, then?'

She counted on her fingers: 'Part-songs. A play-reading. Poetry. Music for five instruments. There are several more things, too, but I've forgotten them. I'll remember in a minute.' She went on laughing.

'Don't bother, that's enough to be going on with. This is really serious. Neddy must be going quite mad at last. It's absolutely crazy. Nobody'll come.'

'You're wrong there, I'm afraid: a fellow from the B.B.C. has promised to come. And a camera team from *Picture Post*. Several of the better-known local musicians will appear, including your friend Johns from the College office with . . .'

Dixon gave a half-voiced howl. 'This can't be right,' he said, emptying his glass despairingly. 'No more dreams, please. They can't fit a crowd like that into the house. Or are they going to sleep on the lawn? And what . . .'

'Most of them are just coming on the Sunday for the day, according to Mrs Neddy. But there will be boarders, as well as you. Johns is arriving on the Friday evening, probably driven here with you. . . .'

'I'll murder the little beast before I get into the same . . .'

'Yes, yes, of course; don't shout. One of the sons is coming too, with his girl. The girl might be rather interesting; a ballet student, I believe.'

'A ballet student? I didn't know there were such things.'

'There are, apparently. This one's called Sonia Loosmore.'

'No, really? How do you know all this?'

'I've heard nothing else from the Neddies for the last week.'

'I can imagine that,' Dixon said. 'Then perhaps you can tell me why I've been asked.'

'Just to join in, I suppose. There'll be plenty of things for you to do, I've no doubt at all.'

'Look, Margaret, you know as well as I do that I can't sing, I can't act, I can hardly read, and thank heaven I can't read music. You'll have to start finding out what Neddy has planned for me. So I can start thinking of reasons for not being able to do it.'

She laid her hand on his. 'You can trust me to be on
your side,' she said in a soft voice. He heard the sigh which
always came before her most frightening statements. She
waited until he had to look at her and said: 'How close
we seem to be tonight, James.' A fat-faced man on the
other side of her turned and stared at her. 'All the barriers
are down at last, aren't they?'

Finding this unanswerable, Dixon gazed at her, slowly
nodding his head. She lowered her eyes and might have
been looking for impurities in her beer. 'It seemed almost
too much to hope for.' After another silence, she went on
in a livelier tone: 'But can't we sit somewhere more . . .
out of the public eye?'

CHAPTER 3

At breakfast the next day Dixon said 'Oh, Bill, I wonder
if you could do me a favour.'

'Depends what it is,' Atkinson said.

'Could you ring me up at this number about eleven on
Sunday morning? I'll be there all right and we'll just have
a little talk about the weather, but if by any chance I am
not there, tell whoever answers that my parents have
arrived suddenly and will I please get back as soon as I can.
There, I've written everything down.'

Atkinson raised his thick eyebrows and studied the back
of the envelope. He gave a wild laugh and stared into
Dixon's face. 'Afraid you won't be able to last out, or
what?'

'It's one of my professor's arty week-ends. I've got to go, but I can't bear the whole of Sunday there.'

'Of course, this sort of music's not intended for an audience, you see,' Welch said as he passed the copies round. 'The fun's all in the singing. Everybody's got a real tune to sing—a real tune,' he repeated violently.

Mrs Welch touched some notes on the piano. 'All right, everybody?'

A sound of sleepy bees filled the air round Dixon as the singers hummed their notes to one another. Mrs Welch rejoined them on the low platform that had been built at one end of the music room, taking up her stand by Margaret, the other soprano. A small unhappy-looking woman with thin brown hair was the only contralto. Next to Dixon was Cecil Goldsmith, a fellow-lecturer of his in the College History Department, whose tenor voice held enough savage power, especially above middle C, to hide whatever noises Dixon might find himself obliged to make. Behind him and to one side were three basses, two of them local musicians, the third Evan Johns.

Dixon ran his eye along the lines of black dots, which seemed to go up and down a good deal, and was able to assure himself that everyone was going to have to sing all the time. He'd had some bad moments twenty minutes ago in some Brahms rubbish which began with ten seconds or so of unsupported tenor—more correctly, of unsupported Goldsmith, who had twice stopped at a hidden interval and left him opening and shutting his mouth in silence. He now cautiously reproduced the note Goldsmith was humming and found the effect pleasing rather than the opposite. Why hadn't they had the manners to ask him if he'd like to join in, instead of driving him up on to this platform thing and forcing sheets of paper into his hand?

The singing began to a wave of Welch's bony finger. Dixon kept his head down, moved his mouth as little as was possible while being unmistakably seen to move it, and looked at the words the others were singing. He stopped at the right moment.

All seemed pleased with the performance and anxious for another of the same sort. 'Yes, well, this next one's rather a well-known one. It's called *Now is the Month of Maying*. Now if you'll all just . . .'

From behind Dixon to the left came laughter bursting unpleasantly through a nose. He glanced round to see Johns's pale face split by a grin. The large eyes with their short eyelashes were fixed on him. 'What's the joke?' he asked. If Johns were laughing at Welch, Dixon was ready to come in on Welch's side.

'You'll see,' Johns said. He went on looking at Dixon. 'You'll see,' he added, grinning.

In less than a minute Dixon did see, and clearly. Instead of the usual four parts, this piece employed five. The third and fourth lines of music had *Tenor I* and *Tenor II* written against them; and there was some babyish fa-la-la-la stuff on the second page with numerous gaps in the individual parts. Even Welch's ear might be expected to record the complete absence of one of the parts in such circumstances. It was much too late now for Dixon to explain that he hadn't really meant it when he'd said, half an hour before, that he could read music 'after a fashion'; much too late to claim to be really a bass. Nothing less than a violent attack of illness could get him out of this.

'You'd better take first tenor, Jim,' Goldsmith said; 'the second's a bit tricky.'

Dixon nodded dully, hardly hearing further laughter

from Johns. Before he could cry out, they were past the
piano business and the humming and into the piece. He
moved his lips to the nonsense of : 'Each with his bonny
lass, a-a-seated on the grass: fa-la-la la, fa-la-la-la-la-la la la-
la . . .' but Welch had stopped waving his finger, was holding it still in the air. The singing died. 'Oh, tenors,' Welch
began; 'I didn't seem to hear . . .'

An irregular knocking on the door at the far end of the
room was at once followed by the bursting-open of this
door and the entrance of a tall man wearing a bright yellow
sports-coat, all three buttons of which were fastened, and
displaying a large beard which came down further on one
side than on the other, half hiding a vine-patterned tie.
Dixon guessed with a rush of joy that this must be the
pacifist painting Bertrand whose arrival with his girl had
been the subject of proud announcements by Welch every
few minutes since tea-time. It was an arrival which must
surely bring annoyance sooner or later, but for the moment
it meant a most welcome rescue from the fearful singing.
Even as Dixon thought this, the senior Welches left their
posts and went to greet their son, followed more slowly by
the others who, perhaps finding the chance of a change
not completely unwelcome, broke into conversation as they
moved. Dixon delightedly lit a cigarette, finding himself
alone: one of the musicians was talking to Margaret; Goldsmith and another musician were talking to Carol, Goldsmith's wife, who'd refused, with enviable firmness, to do
more than sit and listen to the singing from a chair near
the fireplace; Johns was doing something clever at the
piano. Dixon moved down the room through the company
and leaned against the wall at the end by the door where
the bookshelves were. Placed here, enjoying his cigarette,
he was in a good position to observe Bertrand's girl when

she came in, slowly and hesitantly, a few seconds later, and stood unnoticed, except by him, just inside the room.

In a few more seconds Dixon had noticed all he needed to notice about this girl: the combination of fair hair, straight and cut short, with brown eyes and no lipstick, the strict look of the mouth and the square shoulders, the well-developed body with the narrow waist, the intentional simplicity of the wine-coloured skirt and the unornamented white linen blouse. The sight of her seemed an irresistible attack on his own habits, standards, and ambitions: something designed to put him in his place for ever. The idea that women like this were never shown to the public except as the property of men like Bertrand was so familiar to him that it had long ceased to appear an injustice. The huge class that contained Margaret had to provide his own womenfolk: those in whom the intention of being attractive could sometimes be made to get itself confused with attractiveness itself; those with whom a too-tight skirt, a wrong-coloured, or no, lipstick, even an inexpert smile could instantly destroy that illusion beyond apparent hope of renewal. But renewal always came: a new cardigan would somehow make the large feet seem smaller, generosity bring back life to the dead hair, a couple of pints of beer put charm into talk of the London stage or French food.

The girl turned her head and found Dixon staring at her. She drew herself up sharply with all the signs of fright. They looked at each other for a moment, until, just as the top of Dixon's head was beginning to feel uncomfortable, a high, baying voice called 'Ah, there you are, darling. Step this way, if you please, and be introduced to the crowd' and Bertrand marched up the room to meet her, throwing Dixon a brief unfriendly glance. Dixon didn't

like him doing that; the only action he required from
Bertrand was an apology, humbly offered, for his personal
appearance.

Dixon had been too distressed at the sight of Bertrand's
girl to want to be introduced to her, and kept out of the
way for a time; then he moved down and started talking to
Margaret and the musician. Bertrand was in command in
the central group, doing a lot of laughing as he told some
long story; his girl paid him the closest attention as if he
might ask her later to repeat what he had said. Coffee and
cakes, intended to take the place of an evening meal, were
brought in, and getting enough of these for himself and
Margaret kept Dixon fully occupied. Then Welch came up
to him and said, vaguely enough: 'Ah, Dixon, come along
now. I want you to meet my son Bertrand and his . . .
his . . . Come along.'

With Margaret at his side, Dixon was soon standing in
front of the two people Welch wanted him to meet, and
Evan Johns. 'This is Mr Dixon and Miss Peel,' Welch
said, and drew the Goldsmiths away.

Before a silence could fall, Margaret said, 'Are you here
for long, Mr Welch?' and Dixon felt grateful to her for
being there and for always having something to say.

Bertrand's jaws snapped successfully on a piece of food
which had almost escaped. He went on chewing while he
thought. 'I doubt it,' he said at last. 'Upon consideration
I feel it to be my duty to doubt it. There are numerous
affairs in London which are in need of my guiding hand.'
He smiled among his beard, from which he now began
brushing small pieces of cake.

'And how's your work going?' Margaret asked.

Bertrand laughed at this, turning towards his girl, who
also laughed, a clear, musical sound not unlike Margaret's

'*This is Mr Dixon and Miss Peel.*'

tiny silver bells. 'My work?' Bertrand echoed. 'You make it sound like a form of charity. Not that some of our friends would disagree with that description of their labours.'

'What work do you do?' Dixon asked flatly.

'I am a painter. Not, alas, a painter of houses, or I should have been able to make my fortune and retire by now. No, no; I paint pictures. Not, alas again, pictures of trade unionists or town halls or naked women, or I should now be enjoying an even larger fortune. No no; just pictures, mere pictures, pictures full stop. And what work do you do? if, of course, I have permission to ask.'

Dixon hesitated; Bertrand's speech, which had clearly been delivered before, had annoyed him in more ways than he'd have believed possible. Bertrand's girl was looking at him questioningly; her eyebrows, which were darker than her hair, were raised, and she now said, in her rather deep voice: 'Do satisfy our curiosity.' Bertrand's eyes, which seemed to be flatter than the normal eyeball, were also fixed on him.

'I'm one of your father's juniors,' Dixon said to Bertrand, deciding that he mustn't be rude. 'I deal with the Middle Ages for the History Department here.'

'Charming, charming,' Bertrand said, and his girl said: 'You enjoy doing that, do you?'

Welch, Dixon noticed, had rejoined the group and was looking from face to face, obviously looking for a point at which he could enter the conversation. Dixon decided to prevent him from finding it at any cost. He said, quietly but quickly: 'Well, of course, it has its own attraction. I can quite see that it hasn't the sort of glamour of,' he turned to the girl, 'your own occupation.' He must show Bertrand that he had the good manners to include her in the conversation.

She looked up at Bertrand, puzzled. 'But I haven't noticed much glamour around in . . .'

'But surely,' Dixon said, 'I know there must be a lot of hard work and exercise attached to it, but the ballet, well,' he took no notice of warning signs from Margaret, 'there must be plenty of glamour there.'

Bertrand was going red in the face and was leaning towards him, struggling to swallow half a cake and speak. The girl repeated with genuine puzzlement: 'The ballet? But I work in a bookshop. Whatever made you think I . . . ?' Johns was grinning. Even Welch had obviously understood what he'd said. What had he done?

'Look here, Dickinson or whatever your name is,' Bertrand began, 'perhaps you think you're being funny, but I'd rather you stopped it, if you don't mind. Don't want to make a quarrel of it, do we?'

The baying quality of his voice, especially in the final question, together with the way he mixed up parts of his words, made Dixon want to call attention to these faults, also, perhaps, to the peculiarity of his eyes. This might make Bertrand attack him physically—splendid: he was confident of winning any such encounter with an artist— or would Bertrand's pacifism stop him? But in the silence which followed Dixon swiftly decided not to go on. He'd made some mistake about the girl; he mustn't make things any worse. 'I'm very sorry if I've made a mistake, but I had the impression that Miss Loosmore here had some connection with . . .'

He turned to Margaret for aid, but before she could speak Welch, of all people, had come in loudly with: 'Poor old Dixon, ma-ha-ha, must have been confusing this . . . this young lady with Sonia Loosmore, a friend of Bertrand's who disappointed us all rather badly some time ago. I think Bertrand must have thought you were . . . making fun of him or something, Dixon, ba-ha-ha.'

'Well, if he'd taken the trouble to be introduced, this wouldn't have happened,' Bertrand said, still red in the face. 'Instead of which, he . . .'

'Don't worry about it, Mr Dixon,' the girl interrupted. 'It was only a silly little misunderstanding. I can quite see how it happened. My name's Christine Callaghan. Altogether different, you see.'

'Well, I'm . . . thanks very much for seeing it that way. I'm very sorry about it, really I am.'

'No, no, don't let it distress you, Dixon,' Bertrand said, with a glance at his girl. 'If you'll excuse us, I think we might move round among the company.'

They moved off, followed at a distance by Johns, towards the Goldsmith group, and Dixon was left alone with Margaret.

'Here, have a cigarette,' she said. 'You must be needing one. What a pig Bertrand is. He might have realised . . .'

'It was my fault, really,' Dixon said, grateful for tobacco and support. 'I should have been there to be introduced.'

'Yes, why weren't you? But he needn't have made it worse. But that's just like him, I believe.'

'I couldn't bear to meet him. How often have you met him?'

'He came here once before, with the Loosmore girl. I say, it is rather queer, isn't it? He was going to marry the Loosmore girl then, and now here he is with a new popsy. Yes, of course; Neddy made a long speech to me only a couple of days ago about when the Loosmore wedding was to be. So as far as he knew . . .'

'Look, Margaret, can't we go out for a drink? I need

one, and we shan't get one here. It's only just eight; we could be back . . .'

Margaret laughed, so that he could see a large number of her teeth, one of them marked with lipstick. She always made up just a little too heavily. 'Oh, James, you're hopeless,' she said. 'Whatever next? Of course we can't go out; what do you suppose the Neddies would think? Just as their brilliant son's arrived? You'd lose your job in an instant.'

'Yes, you're right, I admit. But I'd give anything for three quick pints of beer.'

'Much better for your pocket not to have them.' She began to laugh again. 'You were wonderful during the singing. Your best performance yet.'

'Don't remind me, please.' Dixon laughed too, trying to forget about beer. It was true that he had only three pounds left in his tin box to last until pay-day, which was nine days away. In the bank he had twenty-eight pounds, but this was a fund he'd started against the chance of being sacked.

'Pretty girl, that Christine What's-her-name,' Margaret said.

'Yes, isn't she?'

'Wonderful figure she's got, hasn't she?'

'Yes.'

'Not often you get a figure as good as that with a good-looking face.'

'No.' Dixon prepared himself for the 'but' that was sure to come.

'Pity she's so very proper, of course. I don't like women of that age who try to act the gracious lady. Bit of a prig, too.'

Dixon, who had already thought the same thing, found

he didn't want to have his ideas supported in this way. 'Oh, I don't know,' he said. 'Can't really tell at this stage.'

This was greeted with the tinkle of tiny bells. 'Ah, you always were one for a pretty face, weren't you?'

A maidservant was now collecting the used china, and the company was moving about. The next part of the evening's entertainment was clearly about to start. Margaret entered into conversation with Carol Goldsmith. This woman, aged about forty, thin, with long straight brown hair, Dixon regarded as one of his allies, though sometimes she made him feel small with her older wisdom.

'Hullo, Jim, how's it going?' she asked in her unusually clear voice.

'Badly. There's at least an hour of musical scraping and blowing in front of us.'

'Yes, that's badly, isn't it. Why do we come to this sort of thing?'

'It would hardly be worth coming just to meet the great painter, would it?' Dixon said, meaning to start a conversation which might help him to forget his embarrassment over the recent Loosmore–Callaghan trouble.

For a reason he didn't then understand, the remark was received with noticeable coldness. Margaret looked at him as if he had broken some law. Carol half-closed her eyes and smoothed her straight hair. 'What makes you say that?' she said.

'Well, nothing really,' Dixon said in alarm. 'I had a little disagreement with him just now, that's all. I got into some mix-up with his girl's name, and he was a bit rude, I thought. Nothing very serious.'

'Oh, that's just like him,' Carol said. 'He always thinks he's being attacked. He often is, too.'

'Oh, you know him, do you?' Dixon said. 'I'm sorry, Carol; is he a great friend of yours?'

A great baying laugh made all three turn round. Bertrand, leading Goldsmith by the arm, was approaching. With the remains of his laughter still trickling from his face, he said to Carol: 'Ah, there you are, dear girl. And how are things with you?'

'Well enough, thank you, dear man. I can see how things are with you. A bit different from your usual, isn't she?'

'Christine? Ah, now there's a fine girl, a fine girl. One of the best, she is. At the moment, quite frankly, she's annoyed me just the tiniest bit,' Bertrand said, showing with his finger and thumb how little the tiniest bit was.

'How did that happen?' Goldsmith asked.

'Well, as you may imagine, in spite of my passionate interest in this kind of sport,' he nodded towards the piano, where the local musicians were making ready, 'it isn't quite enough to draw me down here unaided, glad as I am to see you all. No, no; I had been promised a meeting with a certain Julius Gore-Urquhart, of whom you may have heard.'

Dixon had indeed heard of Gore-Urquhart, a rich lover of the arts who made occasional contributions to the arts sections of the weekly reviews, who had a house in the neighbourhood where distinguished persons sometimes came to stay, and whom Welch had tried in vain to bring to his parties. Dixon looked again at Bertrand's eyes. They really were extraordinary: it seemed as if a sheet of some patterned material were fastened to the inside of his face, showing only at two purposeless holes. What could a man with such eyes, such a beard, and (he noticed them for the first time) such dissimilar ears have to do with a man like Gore-Urquhart?

He learned what they had to do with each other in the next minute or two. The connection was still slight: the Callaghan girl, who knew Gore-Urquhart's family, or was even perhaps his niece, had arranged to introduce Bertrand to him during the week-end. At some late stage it had been found that Gore-Urquhart was at present in Paris, so that a further visit to this part of the country would be necessary in order to meet him. There was some reason, which Dixon at once forgot, why a meeting in London would be less satisfactory. And what was Gore-Urquhart going to do for Bertrand when they did meet?

When Margaret had arrived in her usual roundabout way at a request for this information, Bertrand raised his great head and looked down his cheeks from face to face before replying. 'I have it on more than ordinarily good authority,' he said solemnly, 'that our influential friend will before long be declaring his private secretaryship vacant. I doubt whether the post will be publicly competed for, and so I'm at the moment busy preparing to take the engagement. Patronage, you see, patronage: that's what it'll be. I'll answer his letters with one hand and paint with the other.' He gave a laugh in which Goldsmith and Margaret joined. 'So I'm naturally anxious to strike while the iron's hot, if you'll pardon the expression.'

Why shouldn't they pardon the expression? Dixon thought. Why?

Further conversation was drowned by a long thundering in the bass of the piano. Dixon had begun a question, but Mrs Welch, Margaret, Johns, the Goldsmiths, and the contralto woman all seemed to turn towards him at the same moment. 'Ssshh,' they all said. It was like a railway

engine blowing out steam under a glass roof. Dixon moved
swiftly towards the door. Before he could reach the door,
it opened and Welch entered. 'Oh, you've started, have
you?' he asked without lowering his voice at all.

'Yes,' Dixon whispered, 'I think I'll just . . .'

He shut the door on Welch's long-lived, wondering
frown.

CHAPTER 4

Dixon stopped singing; it was hard work walking up the
dry, sandy track to the Welches' house, especially with so
much beer washing about inside him. A dreamy smile
stretched his face in the darkness. Rebounding painfully
from the gatepost, he began creeping round the stone sur-
roundings of the house.

The large, long room at the back, where the music had
been going on, was in darkness. That was good. But
further round, where the sitting-room was, there were
lights and, he soon found, voices in conversation. Peering
through a narrow gap in the curtains, he saw Welch, in his
red-striped blue raincoat and fishing-hat, just going out of
the door, followed by one of the musicians and Cecil Goldsmith, both of them also dressed in raincoats. People were
evidently about to be driven home; Dixon grinned as he
imagined the sort of drive Welch would give them. Carol,
in a light woollen coat, stayed for a moment to exchange
a last remark with Bertrand. Nobody else was in the room.

A window was open, but Dixon couldn't catch the words
now spoken by Bertrand. He could tell from the tone that

they formed a question to which Carol said: 'Yes, all right.' At this, Bertrand stepped forward and put his arms round her. Dixon couldn't see what followed, because Bertrand had his back to the window, but if there was a kiss it lasted only a moment; Carol freed herself and hurried out. Bertrand went too.

Dixon went back to the music-room and got in through the long window. What he'd seen had disturbed him in some way he couldn't quite understand. To have seen and talked to Cecil Goldsmith several times a week for some months didn't make the fellow any less lacking in personality, but it gave him a claim to one's support, a claim which was somehow called up by the sight of his wife being handled by another man, especially that other man. Dixon wished he hadn't found that gap in the curtains, then put the matter out of his mind. All his attention would be needed for the business of getting up to his bedroom unobserved.

Deciding that the small risk of someone coming into the music-room had got to be taken anyway, Dixon groped through the darkness to a chair, lay back in it, closed his eyes, and heard with satisfaction the sound of Welch's car being started and driven away. After a moment, he felt as if he were rocking over backwards, and the inside of his stomach seemed to swell so as to start enclosing his head inside it. He opened his eyes again, making his tragic-mask face; yes, it had after all been a bad idea to take that last pint. It was time to move.

He creaked up the stairs and along the passage. As a result of some curious building practice, his bedroom could only be approached through a large bathroom, the outer door of which he now tried to open. Nothing happened. The bathroom was evidently occupied. Dixon stood back, legs wide apart, and threatened the door with destruction, before going into a mad dance of rage. Just then somebody opened a door on the other side of the passage. There was no time to do anything at all except try to look like someone waiting outside a bathroom, which was not very effective in the raincoat he still wore.

'James! What on earth are you doing?'

Never had Dixon been so glad to see Margaret rather than anyone else. 'Ssshh,' he said. 'Get me away from here.'

He liked her even more when she beckoned to him and led him, without more words, into her bedroom. Just as he closed the door of this, whoever it was came out of the bathroom. Dixon realised his heart had been beating violently. 'Thank heaven for that,' he said.

'Well, where have you been all the evening, James?'

Whilst he told her he made remarks to himself about the displeasure shown by her expression and manner. What would this sort of thing be like if they ever got married? At the same time he had to admit she looked at her best in the blue dressing-gown, her brown hair loosed from its pins and rolls. He took off his raincoat and lit a cigarette, beginning to feel better. He finished what he had to say without mentioning what he'd seen through the sitting-room window.

After listening to him in silence she smiled slightly. 'Well, I really can't blame you, I suppose. It was rather impolite, all the same. I could see Mrs Neddy thought it was a bit rude.'

'Oh, she thought that it was a bit that, did she? Where did you say I'd gone?'

'I didn't get a chance to say anything: Evan told her he thought you'd probably gone to the pub.'

'I'll kill that little animal before long. That's good, isn't it? Nice friendly spirit. This ought to put me nicely in the wrong with the Neddies. And don't call him Evan.'

'Don't worry too much. Neddy didn't seem to mind.'

'How can you possibly be sure of that? There's no way of telling what goes on inside that head of his, if anything. Just wait a minute, will you? There's something I want to do in the bathroom. Don't go away.'

When he came back she was still sitting on the bed, but had evidently put on some lipstick for him. This pleased him, more because it was a compliment than because of the effect; indeed, he was beginning to feel really good again, and remained so, even leaning back in his chair, while for a few minutes they discussed the early part of the evening. Then Margaret said: 'I say, don't you think you ought to be going? It's getting late.'

He found himself pushed out, his coat over his arm, his head spinning round and round. Half-way to the bathroom he found himself face to face with the Callaghan woman. 'Good evening,' he said politely. She looked away and went past him to her room. He tried to open the bathroom door; it was again locked. Without thinking he threw back his head, filled his lungs, and let loose a loud and prolonged bray of rage. Then he went heavily down the stairs, hung his coat on a hook, went into the dining-room, and bowed in worship in front of the imitation, or possibly genuine, eighteenth-century sideboard.

In a moment he'd taken a bottle of sherry from among the wines and beer which filled half a shelf inside. It was from this bottle that Welch had, the previous evening, poured Dixon the smallest drink he'd ever been seriously offered. He drank deeply. Some of the liquor trickled refreshingly down his chin and under his shirt collar. The bottle had been about three-quarters full when he started, and was about three-quarters empty when he stopped. He pushed it back into position, and, feeling really splendid, reached his bedroom without difficulty.

Here he wandered about for a few minutes, undressing slowly, and presently went into the bathroom tying his pyjama-cord.

Though it was a cool night for early summer, he found he felt hot and was sweating. He stood for some time in front of the wash-basin, trying to discover more about how he felt. His body seemed swollen below the chest. The stuff coming from the light seemed less like light than a very thin but cloudy gas; it gave a creamy hum. He turned on the cold tap and bent over the basin. When he did this, he had to correct an impulse to go on leaning forward until his head lay between the taps. He wetted his face, took a plastic cup from the glass shelf above the basin, and drank a very great deal of water, which refreshed him for a moment, though it had some other effect which he couldn't at once name. He cleaned his teeth with a lot of toothpaste, wetted his face again, refilling the cup, and ate some more toothpaste.

He began getting into bed. His four remaining cigarettes —had he really smoked twelve that evening?—lay in their packet on a polished table at the bed-head, accompanied by matches, the plastic cup of water, and an ash tray. The fact that he was unable for the moment to raise his second foot on to the bed let him know what had been the second effect of drinking all that water: it had made him drunk. He reached up and turned off the light above his head. The room began to rise upwards from the right-hand bottom corner of the bed, and yet seemed to keep in the same position. He threw back the covers and sat on the edge of the bed, his legs hanging. The room settled down to rest. After a few moments he swung his legs back and lay down. The room lifted. He put his feet on the floor. The room stayed still. He put his legs on the bed but didn't lie down. The room moved. He sat on the edge of the bed. Nothing. He put one leg up on the bed. Something. In fact a great deal. Swearing, he heaped up the pillows, half-lay, half-sat against them, and hung his legs half-over the edge of the bed. In this position he was able to lower himself slowly and carefully into sleep.

CHAPTER 5

Dixon was alive again. Consciousness attacked him before he could get out of the way. A dusty thudding in his head made the scene in front of his eyes beat like a pulse. His mouth. . . . He felt bad.

He reached out for and put on his glasses. At once he saw that something was wrong with the bedclothes straight in front of his face. Risking everything, he sat up a little and what met his bursting eyes sent the big-drummer in his head mad. A large irregular area of the turned-back part of the sheet was missing; a smaller but still noticeable area of the turned-back part of the blanket was also missing; an area about the size of his hand in the main part of the top blanket was missing. Through the three holes, which, fitly enough, had black borders, he could see a dark brown mark on the second blanket. He ran a finger round a bit of the hole in the sheet, and when he looked at his

finger it bore a dark-grey stain. That meant ash; ash meant
burning; burning must mean cigarettes. Had his cigarette
burnt itself out on the blanket? If not, where was it now?
Nowhere on the bed; nor in it. He leaned over the side,
suffering; a brown channel, ending in a tiny piece of dis-
coloured paper, lay across a light patch in the pattern of a
valuable-looking rug. This made him feel very unhappy, a
feeling greatly increased when he looked at the bedside
table. This was marked by two black, pencil-shaped hollows
some distance from the ash tray, which held a single used
match. On the table were two unused matches; the rest lay
with the empty cigarette packet on the floor. The plastic
cup was nowhere to be seen.

Had he done all this himself? He must have. Surely this
would mean the loss of his job, especially if he failed to go
to Mrs Welch and confess what he'd done, and he knew
already that he wouldn't be able to do that. There was no
excuse which didn't consist of the inexcusable: an incendiary was no more pardonable when revealed as a drunkard
as well—so much of a drunkard, too, that his duty to his
hosts and fellow-guests and the attraction of fine music
were as nothing compared with the temptation of drink.

He got out of bed and went into the bathroom. After a
minute or two he returned, eating toothpaste and carrying
a safety-razor blade. He started carefully cutting round
the edges of the burnt areas of the bedclothes with the
blade. He didn't know why he did this, but the operation
did seem to improve the look of things: the cause of the
disaster wasn't so obvious. When all the edges were smooth
and regular, he knelt down slowly, as if he'd suddenly
become a very old man, and shaved the damaged part of
the rug. The bits and pieces from these improvements he
pushed into his pyjama pocket, thinking that he'd have a

He made irregular cuts into the material.

bath and then go downstairs and telephone Atkinson and ask him to be earlier than had been arranged with his message about the senior Dixons.

He was all ready to creep down to the telephone when, returning to the bedroom, he again studied the ruined bedclothes. They looked in some way unsatisfactory; he couldn't have said how. He went and locked the outer bathroom door, picked up the razor-blade, and began again to work on the edges of the holes. This time he made irregular cuts into the material. Then he held the blade against the edges and ran it quickly round the holes to make a rough appearance. That was much better, he decided. The disaster now seemed much less obviously the work of man and might, for a few seconds, be thought to be caused by some violent form of rot or the attacks of a colony of moths. He turned the rug round so that the shaved burn, without being actually hidden by a chair, was not far from it. He was considering taking the bedside table downstairs and later throwing it out of the bus on his journey back when a familiar voice came to his ears, singing in a way that suggested careless joy. The bathroom door was shaken. Then the singing stopped, but the shaking went on, was joined by kicking and even by the thudding of what must be a shoulder. Welch hadn't thought in advance that the bathroom might be occupied by another; nor did he soon realise it now. The shaking, knocking and thudding went on for minutes before he gave up and returned to his room.

Dixon left the bedroom, first unintentionally standing on and destroying the plastic cup, which must have rolled out from under something into his path. Downstairs he looked at the hall clock—twenty past eight—and went into the sitting-room, where the telephone was. It was fortunate that Atkinson got up early on Sundays to go out for the newspapers. He picked up the telephone.

What gave him most trouble during the next twenty-five minutes was finding some outlet for his feelings without hurting his head too much. Nothing at all came out of the telephone receiver during that time except the faint whispering of some unknown sea. He gave up and left.

The only person in the breakfast-room was the Callaghan girl, sitting behind a well-filled plate. Dixon said good morning to her.

'Oh, good morning.' Her tone was neutral, not hostile.

He quickly decided on a man-to-man, speak-my-mind approach as the best cover for rudeness, past or to come. Speaking on purpose with a stronger northern pronunciation than usual, Dixon said: 'I'm afraid I made a bad start when we met last night.'

She looked up quickly, and he saw with bitterness how pretty her neck was. 'Oh . . . that. I shouldn't worry too much about it if I were you. I didn't show up too well myself.'

'Nice of you to see it that way,' he said, remembering that he'd already had reason to say something of that sort to her. 'Very bad mannered of me, in any case.'

'Well, let's forget it, shall we?'

'Glad to; thanks very much.'

There was a pause, while he noticed with some surprise how much and how quickly she was eating. A study of the plateful of food opposite him made him decide to postpone eating any himself. His throat and stomach felt as if they were being neatly sewn up as he sat. He poured and drank a cup of coffee, then filled his cup again.

'Aren't you going to have any of this stuff?' the girl asked.

'Well, not yet, I don't think.'

'What's the matter? Aren't you feeling very well?'

'No, not really, I must admit. Bit of a headache, you know.'

'Oh, then you did go to the pub, as that little man said what was his name?'

'Johns,' Dixon said, trying to suggest by the way he said the name the correct opinion of its bearer. 'Yes, I did go to the pub.'

'You had a lot, did you?' In her interest she stopped eating, but still kept hold of her knife and fork. He noticed that her fingers were square-topped, with the nails cut quite short.

'I suppose I must have done, yes," he replied.

'How much did you have?'

'Ooh . . . seven or eight, possibly.'

'Pints of beer?'

'Yes.' He smiled slightly, thinking she didn't seem so bad after all, and that the slight blueness of the whites of her eyes helped to give her a look of health. He changed his mind about the first of these observations, and lost interest in the second, when she replied:

'Well, if you drink as much as that you must expect to feel a bit unwell the next day, mustn't you?' She drew herself upright in her chair in a very schoolmarmy attitude.

Suddenly he remembered the bedclothes; how could he have been such a fool? He couldn't possibly leave them like that. He must do something else to them. He must get up to his room quickly and look at them and see what their appearance suggested. 'Help,' he said to himself, then to her: 'I'm afraid I've got to go upstairs.' Realising that this did not sound very good, he said wildly: 'There's something wrong with my room—something I must change.' He looked at her and saw her eyes were wide with interest. 'I had a fire last night.'

'You lit a fire in your bedroom?'

'No, I didn't light it purposely. I lit it with a cigarette. It caught fire by itself.'

Her expression changed again. 'Your bedroom caught fire?'

'No, only the bed. I lit it with a cigarette.'

'You mean you set fire to your bed?'

'That's right.'

'With a cigarette? Not meaning to? Why didn't you put it out?'

'I was asleep. I didn't know about it till I woke up.'

'But you must have. . . . Didn't it burn you?'

'It doesn't seem to have done.'

'Oh, well, that's good, at least.' She looked at him with her lips pressed firmly together, then laughed in a way quite different from the way she'd laughed the previous evening; in fact, Dixon thought, rather unmusically. It made some of the devotedly-brushed blonde hair fall forward, and she smoothed it back. 'Well, what are you going to do?'

'I don't know yet. But I must do something.'

'Yes, I quite agree. You'd better start on it quickly, hadn't you, before the maid goes round?'

'I know. But what can I do?'

'How bad is it?'

'Bad enough. There are great pieces gone altogether, you see.'

'Oh. I don't know what to suggest without seeing it. Unless you . . . no; that wouldn't help.'

'Look, I suppose you wouldn't come up and . . . ?'

'Have a look at it?'

'Yes. Do you think you could?'

She sat up again and thought. 'Yes, all right. I don't promise anything, of course.'

'No, of course not.' He remembered with joy that he still had some cigarettes left after last night's happenings. 'Thanks very much.'

They went quietly through the hall and up the stairs. Dixon found, with sharp relief, that he could open the bathroom door.

The girl looked sternly at him. 'What are we going in here for?'

'My bedroom's on the far side of this.'

'Oh, I see. What a curious arrangement.'

'I imagine old Welch had parts of this house built on. It's better like this than having the bathroom on the far side of a bedroom.'

'I suppose so. My goodness, you certainly have had a party, haven't you?' She went forward and fingered the sheet and blankets like one shown material in a shop. 'But this doesn't look like a burn; it looks as if it's been cut with something.'

'Yes, I . . . cut the burnt bits off with a razor-blade. I thought it would look better than just leaving it burnt.'

'Why on earth did you do that?'

'I can't really explain. I just thought it would look better.'

'Mm. And did all this come from one cigarette?'

'I don't know. Probably.'

'Well, you must have been in a bad state not to . . . And the table too. And the rug. You know, I don't know that I ought to have any part in all this.' She grinned, which made her look almost ridiculously healthy, and revealed at the same time that her front teeth were slightly

irregular. For some reason this was more disturbing to his
balance of mind than regularity could possibly have been.
He began to think he'd noticed quite enough things about
her now, thank you. Then she drew herself up and pressed
her lips together, seeming to consider. 'I think the best
thing would be to remake the bed with all this at the
bottom, out of sight. We can put the blanket that's only
got a brown mark—this one—on top; it'll probably be
almost all right on the side that's underneath now. Is that
all right?'

'Yes. Sounds all right to me. But they're bound to find
it when they change all the bedclothes, aren't they?'

'Yes, but they probably won't connect it with smoking,
especially after what you did with your razor-blade. And
after all, you wouldn't have put your head right down to
the bottom of the bed to smoke, would you?'

'That's true, of course. We'd better start, then.'

He pulled the bed away from the wall, while she watched
with arms folded, then they both began the work of
unmaking and remaking. As they worked, Dixon studied
the Callaghan girl, in spite of his determination to notice
nothing more about her, and saw with fury that she was
prettier than he'd thought. The girl was guilty—doubly
guilty, first of looking like that, secondly of appearing in
front of him looking like that.

'There. I think that looks very nice,' the girl said. 'You
couldn't guess what was underneath at all if you didn't
know, could you?'

'No, and thanks very much for the idea and the help.'

'Oh, that's all right. What are you going to do with the
table?'

'I've been thinking about that. There's a little storeroom at the end of the passage, full of broken furniture and

rotting books and things. They sent me up there yesterday to fetch a music-stand or what ever they call the things. See whether there's anyone in the passage. I'll rush along there with it now.'

'Agreed. I must say that's an inspiration. With the table gone, nobody'll connect the sheets with smoking. They'll think you tore them with your feet, in a terrible dream or something.'

'Quite a dream—to get through two blankets as well.'

She looked at him open-mouthed, then began to laugh. She sat down on the bed but immediately jumped up again as if it were once more on fire. Dixon began laughing too, not because he was much amused but because he felt grateful to her for her laughter. They were still laughing a minute later when she beckoned to him from outside the bathroom door, when he ran out into the passage with the table, and when Margaret suddenly threw open the door of her bedroom and saw them.

'What do you imagine you're doing, James?' she asked.

CHAPTER 6

'We're just . . . I'm just . . . I was just getting rid of this table, as a matter of fact,' Dixon said, looking from one woman to the other.

The Callaghan girl gave an extraordinarily loud snort, trying to hold back her laughter. Margaret said: 'Just what is all this nonsense?'

'It isn't nonsense, Margaret, I assure you. I've . . .'

'If nobody minds my saying so,' the girl interrupted

him, 'I think we'd better get rid of the table first and explain the whys and wherefores afterwards, don't you?'

'That's right,' Dixon said, put his head down, and ran up the passage. In the storeroom he pushed aside all sorts of rubbish and put the table behind an old screen. He found an old cloth to put on it and then arranged an interesting composition of old rubbish on top. The effect, when he stepped back to look, was excellent; no observer could doubt that these objects had lived together for years in just this way. He smiled, shutting his eyes for a moment before spilling back into the world of reality.

Margaret was waiting for him at the door of her room. One corner of her mouth was drawn in in a way he knew well. The Callaghan girl had gone.

'Well, what was all that about, James?'

He shut the door and began to explain. As he talked, his incendiarism and what had been done to hide it struck him for the first time as funny. Surely Margaret, especially as she wasn't personally involved, must find it funny too; it made the sort of story she liked. He said so at the end of his account.

Without changing her expression, she disagreed. 'But I could see that you and that girl were finding it very funny.'

'Well, why shouldn't we have found it funny?'

'No reason at all; it's nothing to do with me. The whole thing just strikes me as rather silly and childish, that's all.'

Some time later a loud baying howl of 'Dixon' brought him to the top of the stairs. 'Somebody want me?' he roared.

'Telephone. Dixon. Dixon. Telephone.'

In the sitting-room, Bertrand was talking to his parents

and his girl. He pointed to the telephone with his big head and went on talking.

'That you, Jim?' said Atkinson's cruel voice. 'How are you getting along at the circus?'

'All the better for hearing your voice, Bill.'

While Atkinson, unexpectedly ready to talk, described a court case he'd been reading about in his Sunday newspaper and then made a not very practical suggestion for the entertainment of the company at the Welches', Dixon watched the Callaghan girl listening to something Bertrand was explaining about art. She was sitting straight upright in her chair, her lips pressed together, wearing, he noticed for the first time, exactly what she'd been wearing the previous evening. She looked severe in every way, and yet she didn't mind sheets and burnt table-tops, and Margaret did.

Raising his voice a little, Dixon said: 'Well, thanks very much for telephoning, Bill. Apologise to my parents, will you, and tell them I'll be back as soon as I can?'

He waited until Bertrand stopped talking for a moment and then said: 'I'm afraid I shall have to leave at once, Mrs Welch. That telephone call . . .'

They all looked round at him, Bertrand impatiently, Mrs Welch as if he had done something wrong, Welch without any understanding, Bertrand's girl without any curiosity.

He tried again: 'I'm afraid I've got to go now. My parents have come to see me unexpectedly.' He paused to give time for any cries of protest and regret. When none came, he hurried on: 'Thank you very much for everything, Mrs Welch; I've enjoyed myself very much. And now I'm afraid I really must go. Good-bye, everybody.'

He walked through the silence and out of the door.

CHAPTER 7

The examinations were now in progress, and Dixon had nothing to do during the morning except to be at the Assembly Hall at twelve-thirty to collect some answer papers. They would contain answers to questions he'd set about the Middle Ages. As he approached the Common Room he thought briefly about the Middle Ages. Those who claimed that they were unable to believe in the reality of human progress ought to cheer themselves up, as the students now being examined had perhaps been cheered up, by a short study of the Middle Ages. The hydrogen bomb, the South African Government, Chiang Kai-shek, the latest troublesome politicians, would all seem a light price to pay for no longer being in the Middle Ages. Had people ever been as nasty, as greedy, as dull, as miserable, as sure of themselves, as bad at art, as sadly ridiculous, or as wrong as they'd been in the Middle Ages?

In the Common Room he caught sight of Margaret, pale and heavy-eyed, sitting alone near the empty fireplace. Their relations hadn't changed much during the ten days since the arty week-end. It had taken him a whole evening in the Royal Hotel and a great deal of expense and hypocrisy to get her to admit that she still had a feeling of displeasure with him, and more of the same sorts of expense to persuade her to explain the displeasure, discuss it, reduce it, and finally abandon it. For some reason, noticeable from time to time but impossible to name, the sight of her now filled him with affectionate remorse. Taking an orange drink instead of coffee, because it was a hot day, he ·went through the talking groups over to Margaret. 'Hullo, dear, how are you today?' he said.

'All right, thanks.'

He risked a smile. 'You don't sound as though you mean that.'

'Don't I? I'm sorry. I'm quite all right really.' She spoke with extraordinary sharpness. Her jaw-muscles looked tight, as if she was suffering from toothache.

Glancing round him, he moved closer, bent forward, and said as gently as he could: 'Now, Margaret, please don't talk like that. It's quite unnecessary. If you don't feel very well, tell me about it and I'll sympathise. If you feel all right, that's fine. In any case we'll smoke a cigarette together. But for heaven's sake don't try to start a quarrel with me. I don't feel like one.'

She made a sudden movement on the chair-arm she was sitting on so that her back was towards everybody in the room except Dixon, who saw that her eyes were filling with tears. As he hesitated, she gave a loud sob, still looking at him.

'Margaret, you mustn't,' he said in horror. 'Don't cry. I didn't mean it.'

She gave a furious downward movement of her hand. 'You were quite right,' she said, trembling violently. 'It was my fault, I'm sorry.'

'Margaret . . .'

'No. I'm the one in the wrong. I snapped at you. I didn't want to; I didn't mean to. Everything's so awful this morning.'

'Well, tell me about it, then. Dry your eyes.'

'You're the only one that's nice to me and then I treat you like that.' But she took off her glasses and started pushing a handkerchief into her eyes.

'Never mind about that. Tell me what's wrong.'

'Oh, nothing. Everything and nothing.'

'Did you have another bad night?'

'Yes, darling, I did, and it's made me terribly sorry for myself, as usual. I keep thinking to myself, Oh hell, what's the use of anything, especially me?'

'Have a cigarette.'

'Oh, thank you, James; it's just what I want. Do I look all right?'

'Yes, of course. Just a little tired, that's all.'

'I couldn't go to sleep until after four. I must go and see the doctor and ask him to give me something. I can't go on like this.'

They talked like this for a few minutes, while the other people in the room began to go out to their various duties. There was one piece of news which Margaret gave him that interested Dixon. Bertrand was going to take Carol Goldsmith to the College Summer Ball, her husband being obliged to go to Leeds as Welch's representative for the week-end. It must be supposed, then, that Bertrand's blonde and well-built Callaghan popsy had now, to her credit, been dropped. The interest of this situation took most of the sting out of the probability that Carol, Bertrand, Margaret, and himself would be going to the Ball together; 'as a little party,' Margaret had said.

CHAPTER 8

'Professor Welch. Professor Welch, please.'

Dixon tried to hide behind the magazine he was reading and secretly made his man-from-Mars face. To him, it was a serious offence to pronounce that name in public, even when there was no danger that it would cause its bearer to appear; Welch was known to be staying away for the whole day, as distinct from days like yesterday when Welch merely stayed away for the early and late morning and the afternoon. Dixon wished that the porter, a very bad man, would stop braying that particular name and go away before his eye fell on Dixon and took notice of him as a Welch-creature. But it was no good; in a moment he felt the approach of the porter through the length of the Common Room towards his chair, and had to look up.

The porter wore a dark-green uniform of military cut, and an official cap which didn't suit him. He was a long-faced, high-shouldered man with hairs growing out of his nose, and his age was hard to estimate. His expression, which seldom changed, couldn't be expected to at the sight of Dixon. Still approaching, he said through the sand in his throat: 'Oh, Mr. Jackson.'

Dixon wished he had the courage to twist eagerly around in his chair in search of this quite new and unknown character. 'Yes, Maconochie?' he said helpfully.

'Oh, Mr. Jackson, there's someone on the telephone for Professor Welch, but I can't find him. Would you take the call for him, please? You're the only person in the History Department I can find,' he explained.

'Yes, all right,' Dixon said. 'Can I take it in here?'

'Thank you, Mr. Jackson. No, the telephone in here goes to the public exchange. The lady wanting the Professor's on the College switchboard. I'll switch her through to the clerk's office. He won't mind your taking it in there.'

Luckily the clerk, another very bad man, wasn't in his room. Dixon picked up the telephone and said: 'Dixon here. Can I take a message for Professor Welch?'

'Oh, Mr. Dixon.' There was a noise which might have

been failure to stop a burst of laughter. 'I might have guessed it'd be you. This is Christine Callaghan.'

'Oh, hullo, er, how are you?' Recognition brought a feeling that his inside had become liquid, but it lasted only a moment; he knew that he could deal with her voice well enough while the rest of her remained, as he supposed, in London.

'I'm very well, thanks. How are you? I hope you've had no more trouble with your bed-clothes?'

Dixon laughed. 'No, I'm glad to say that's all over—I hope.'

'Oh, good. . . . I say, is it at all possible for me to speak to Professor Welch, do you know? Isn't he anywhere in the University?'

'He hasn t been here all the morning, I'm afraid. He's almost certainly at home now. Or have you tried there?'

'Oh, how annoying! Perhaps you can tell me: do you know if he's expecting a visit from Bertrand?'

'Well, yes, as it happens, I do know that Bertrand's coming at the week-end. Margaret Peel told me.' Dixon's calm had departed; evidently this girl didn't know she'd been dropped by Bertrand, at least as far as the Summer Ball was concerned. Answering her questions about Bertrand was going to be difficult.

'Who told you?' Her voice had sharpened a little.

'You know, Margaret Peel. The girl who was staying with the Welches when you came that time.'

'Oh yes, I see. . . . Did she happen to mention whether Bertrand will be going to your Summer Ball?'

Dixon thought quickly; no questions about Bertrand s possible partner must be asked. 'No, I'm afraid not. But everybody else'll be going.' Why didn't she telephone Bertrand and ask him?

'I see. . . . But he is definitely coming?'

'Apparently.'

She must have realised that he was puzzled, because she now said: 'I expect you're wondering why I don't ask Bertrand himself. Well, you see, he's often rather difficult to find. At the moment he's just gone off, nobody knows where. He likes to come and go when he feels like it; hates being tied down. Do you see?'

'Yes, of course.' Dixon made walking legs with the first two fingers of his free hand.

'So I thought I'd find out whether his father knew where he was or anything. What I really wanted to know is this. My Uncle, Mr Gore-Urquhart, got back from Paris sooner than he expected, and he's got an invitation from your Principal to the Summer Ball. He doesn't really know whether to come or not. Well, I could persuade him to come if Bertrand and I were going, and then Bertrand and he could meet each other, and Bertrand wants that. But I must know soon, because it's the day after tomorrow and Uncle would want to know where he's to spend the week-end, I mean. So . . . well, it's rather a mix-up, I'm afraid.'

'Can't Mrs Welch give you any information?'

There was a pause. 'I haven't actually asked her.'

'Well, she's sure to know more about it than I do, isn't she? . . . Hullo?'

'I'm still here. . . . Listen, don't tell anyone, will you? but I'd like not to ask her if I can find any other way. I . . . we didn't get along with each other very well when I was there. I don't want to have to, well, discuss Bertrand with her on the telephone. I think she thinks I'm . . . Never mind; but you see what I mean?'

'I do indeed. I don't get along with the lady, either, as

a matter of fact. Now I've a suggestion. I'll ring up the Welches for you now and ask the Professor to telephone you. If he's not there I'll give a message or something. In any case I'll arrange somehow that Mrs Welch isn't involved. If I don't succeed I'll ring you up myself and and tell you. Will that be all right?'

'Oh, that'd be wonderful. Thank you very much. What a marvellous idea. Here's my number; it's the place I work at, so I shan't be there after five-thirty. Ready?'

While he wrote it down, Dixon assured himself several times that Mrs Welch couldn't have found out about the sheet or the table, or Margaret would surely have warned him. How nice this girl was being to him, he thought. 'Right, I've got that,' he said finally.

'It's wonderful of you to do this for me,' the girl said eagerly. 'But doesn't it make me look rather a fool, your taking all this trouble just to save me . . . ?'

'Not in the least. I know exactly what these things are like.' And that is true, he told himself.

'Will you be going to the Ball?'

'Yes, I'm afraid so.'

'Afraid so?'

'Well, I'm not really a dancing man, you know. It'll be rather unpleasant for me, I'm afraid.'

'Why on earth are you going, then?'

'It's too late to avoid it.'

'What?'

'I said I may be able to enjoy it.'

'Oh, I expect you will. I'm not much good as a dancer myself, really. I've never learnt properly.'

'You must have had plenty of practice, surely.'

'Not much, as a matter of fact. I haven't been to many dances.'

'We'll be able to sit out together, then.' That's rather bold, he thought; I shouldn't have said that.'

'If I come.'

'Yes, if you come.'

'Well, thank you again for your help.'

'Not at all. I hope very much you will be coming on Saturday.'

'I hope so too. Well, good-bye. I may get a telephone call from you later, then.'

'That's right. Good-bye.'

Dixon went back to the Common Room, which was now empty, and sat down at the telephone.

Things happened very quickly. Mrs Welch said to him: 'Celia Welch speaking.'

He'd forgotten about Mrs Welch. But why worry? In an almost normal voice he said: 'Can I speak to Professor Welch, please?'

'That's Mr Dixon, isn't it? Before I get my husband, I'd just like you to tell me, if you don't mind, what you did to the sheet and blankets on your bed when you . . .'

He wanted to scream. His fevered eyes fell on a copy of the local paper that lay on the table. Without stopping to think, he said, changing his voice by making his lips into an O: 'No, Mrs Welch, there must be some mistake. This is the *Evening Post* speaking. There's no Mr. Dixon with us, I'm quite sure.'

'Oh, I'm very very sorry; you sounded at first just like . . . How ridiculous of me.'

'Quite all right, Mrs Welch. Quite all right.'

'I'll get my husband for you immediately.'

'Well, actually it was Mr Bertrand Welch I wanted to speak to really,' Dixon said, smiling at his own cunning as

'It was Mr Bertrand Welch I wanted to speak to really.'

well as he could with his special mouth; in a few seconds this horror would be over.

'I'm not sure whether he's . . . Just wait a minute.' She put the telephone down.

Better wait, Dixon thought. The information which Mrs Welch had obviously gone to get, about where Bertrand could be reached, was just what he wanted for the Callaghan girl. He'd be able to ring her up and tell her, too. Yes, wait at any cost.

The cost came immediately in the form of a well-remembered voice baying loudly into his ear 'This is Bertrand Welch', so loudly, indeed, that Dixon could have imagined that Bertrand was actually in the room with him and had by some magic trick replaced the receiver by those rosy, bearded lips.

'*Evening Post* here,' he managed to get out through his O.

'And what can I do for you, sir?'

Dixon recovered slightly. 'Er . . . we'd like to do a little paragraph about you for our, for our Saturday paper,' he said, beginning to plan. 'That is if you've no objection.'

'Objection? Objection? What objection would a humble painter have to a little harmless publicity? At least, I suppose it's harmless?'

'Oh, quite harmless, I assure you, sir. We have a few facts about you already, of course. But we would just like to know what you're doing at the moment, you see.'

'Of course, of course, very reasonable. Well, I'm working on two or three things just now.' And the baying voice went on for several minutes about the two or three things.

'I see. Well, that'll help us a great deal, Mr. Welch,' Dixon said. Now was the moment for a daring change of subject. 'The young lady said something about an exhibition, sir. Is that right?'

'Yes, I am having a little show locally in the autumn; but what young lady is this?'

Dixon laughed silently with relief through his O. 'A Miss Callaghan, sir,' he said. 'I believe you know her.'

'Yes, I know her,' Bertrand said in a slightly hardened voice. 'Why, where is she concerned in this?'

'Why, I thought you must know,' Dixon said with pretended surprise. 'This was really her idea. She knows one of our staff, and I understand she suggested this little paragraph, so to speak, to him, you see, sir.'

'Really? Well, it's the first I've heard about it. Are you quite sure?'

Dixon gave a quite professional laugh. 'Oh, we don't make mistakes about things like that, sir; it would be extremely dangerous in our position, if you understand me, Mr Welch.'

'Yes, I suppose it would be, but it all sounds most . . .'

'Well, I think you should check with her then, sir, if you're in any doubt. As a matter of fact, when Miss Callaghan was on the telephone to Atkinson . . .'

'Who's this Atkinson? I don't know him.'

'Our Mr Atkinson in the London Office, sir. She was speaking to him only an hour ago, sir, and asked us to ask you to ring her up, if we could get in touch with you. It seems she couldn't get through to your house, or something. Something rather urgent seems to have come up, and she'd like you to ring her up this afternoon, before five-thirty, if you don't mind.'

'All right, I'll do that, then. Oh yes. What's your name in case I . . . ?'

'Barclay, sir,' Dixon said without hesitation. 'Alfred R. Barclay.'

'Right, thank you, Mr Barclay.' (That's the tone, Dixon thought to himself.) 'Oh, I say, when will the paragraph appear?'

'Ah, now that is a difficult question, sir. One just can't be sure, I'm afraid. But it'll certainly be within the next four weeks. We like to have the material ready in plenty of time, you see, Mr. Welch.'

'Yes, of course, yes. Well, have you got all the information you want?'

'Yes, thank you very much indeed, sir.'

'No, no, thanks to you, old boy,' Bertrand said with a welcome return to his earlier friendliness. 'Very fine body of men, the gentlemen of the Press.'

'Nice of you to say so, sir,' Dixon said, making his nasty smell face into the telephone. 'Well, good-bye and thanks, Mr Welch. Very grateful to you.'

'Good-bye, Barclay, old boy.'

Dixon sat back, wiped his face with his handkerchief, though he'd have liked to wipe his whole body, and lit a cigarette. Fright had made him dangerously bold, but not, he thought, beyond the point where he could be saved. The key to the situation lay in making the Callaghan girl understand what was happening before Bertrand found out the truth from her.

Once again he picked up the telephone, asked for a trunk call and then gave Christine Callaghan's number. Better not tell her the full story of his conversation with Bertrand, he thought. When the moment came he leaned forward and said: 'Miss Callaghan? Good. It's Dixon here. Now listen carefully.'

CHAPTER 9

The strain of dancing, always great, and of keeping his eyes on Margaret's face as it bobbed and advanced and moved away, made the speaking of more than a word at a time difficult for Dixon. In addition, he had to keep straining his ears to catch the beat of the music above the noise of many feet and many conversations.

Margaret was talking eagerly; her face was slightly pink, and her lipstick had been more carefully applied than usual. She seemed to be enjoying herself; she looked, as she sometimes could, almost pretty. 'Mr Gore-Urquhart seems very charming, something quite exceptional these days. He's got the most beautiful manners, hasn't he?'

Dixon made a noise in his throat, but before he had time to reply the dance came to an end. He gave a sigh of relief and wiped his hands on his handkerchief. 'Would you like a drink?' he said.

Margaret was darting her eyes this way and that. 'Wait a minute. I just want to see if I can see the others. Ah, here they are,' she said.

Bertrand and Christine were approaching. Bertrand, Dixon had to admit, did not look too bad in evening clothes, and to say now that he looked like an artist of some sort would have been true without being offensive. It was on him that Dixon fixed his eye, less from interest than to avoid fixing it on Christine. Her manner to him so far that evening had been not even cold; it had simply made him feel that, contrary to the evidence of his senses, he wasn't really there at all. But, worse than this, she was looking her best this evening. She wore a yellow dress that left her shoulders bare. It was quite plain, managing, as

55

if it had been intended just for that, to reveal as decidedly
lacking in taste Margaret's blue thing with its bows and
lace, and with the four rows of pearls above it. Christine's
aim, he imagined, had been to show the natural beauty of
her skin. The result had been painfully successful, making
everybody else look like badly developed photographs.
For a moment, as she and Bertrand approached, she gave
Dixon a glance. Although her eyes gave him nothing, he
wanted to pull the collar of his dinner-jacket over his head
and run out into the street.

'Well, people, what is our next entertainment?' Bertrand
asked. He was holding Christine's wrist between finger and
thumb, perhaps taking her pulse. He glanced at Dixon, to
whom he'd so far been fairly friendly.

'Well, I thought we might go and have a drink,' Dixon
said.

'Oh, do be quiet, James; anybody'd think you'd die if
you had to live without one for an hour.'

'He probably would,' Bertrand said. 'In any case, it's
sensible of him not to want to take the risk. Would you
like a drink, darling? I'm afraid there's only beer and fruit
drinks, unless you want to adventure out to some house
of refreshment.'

'Yes, all right, but where's Uncle Julius and Mrs Goldsmith? We can't go away and leave them.'

They went to the bar, a small room not designed for the
purpose. Gore-Urquhart and Carol were sitting at a table
among some quite healthy-looking palms growing in pots,
talking hard. When he saw the others coming towards
them, Gore-Urquhart rose to his feet. This formality was
so unfamiliar in the circles Dixon normally moved in that
for a moment he wondered whether the others meant to
oppose their approach by physical force. He was younger

than Dixon had expected any distinguished man, and an uncle of Christine's, to be: about forty-nine perhaps. His evening suit, too, was not nearly as noticeably 'faultless' as might have been expected. His large smooth face, on top of a short thin body, was of the most irregular shape that Dixon had ever seen.

'I've managed to avoid your Principal so far,' Gore-Urquhart said with his strong Lowland-Scottish pronunciation when they were seated.

'That can't have been easy, Mr Gore-Urquhart,' Margaret said with a laugh. 'I'm sure he's got all his spies out for you.'

'Do you think so, now? Will I be able to get away again if he catches me?'

'Very unlikely, sir,' Bertrand said. 'You know what they're like in this part of the world. Give them a celebrity and they'll fight over him like dogs over a bone. Why, even in my small way I've had a good deal of that sort of thing to endure, especially from university "society". Just because my father happens to be a professor, they think I must want to talk to the Principal's wife about the difficulties her miserable grandson's having at his school. But, of course, it must be a thousand times worse for you, sir; am I right?'

Gore-Urquhart, who'd been listening to this with attention, said briskly 'In some ways', and drank from his glass.

'In any case, Mr Gore-Urquhart,' Margaret said, 'you're quite safe for the moment. The Principal holds court on these occasions in a room at the other end of the dance-floor—he doesn't mix with the common crowd in here.'

'So while I'm with the common crowd I'm fairly safe,

you mean, Miss Peel? Good; I'll stay with the common crowd.'

Dixon had been expecting a silver-bells laugh from Margaret to greet this remark, but it was still hard to bear when it came. At that moment Maconochie arrived with the drinks Gore-Urquhart had ordered. To Dixon's surprise and delight, the beer was in pint glasses and, after waiting for Gore-Urquhart's 'Find me some cigarettes, lad,' to Maconochie, he leaned forward and said: 'How on earth did you manage to get pints? I haven't seen anything but half-pints in here the whole evening. I thought it must be a rule of the place. They wouldn't give me pints when I asked for them. How on earth did you manage it?' While he said this he saw with some annoyance that Margaret was looking from him to Gore-Urquhart and back again and smiling with mild disapproval as if to assure Gore-Urquhart that, in spite of evidence to the contrary, his speech was not really a sign of an unbalanced mind. Bertrand, too, was watching and grinning.

Gore-Urquhart, who didn't seem to have noticed Margaret's smiles, jerked a tobacco-stained thumb towards the departing Maconochie. 'A fellow Scottish Nationalist,' he said.

All the people facing Dixon and to his left—Gore-Urquhart himself, Bertrand and Margaret—laughed at this, and so did Dixon, who looked to his right and saw Christine, sitting next to him with her elbows on the table, smiling in a controlled way, and beyond her Carol, at Gore-Urquhart's left, staring with rather hard eyes at Bertrand. Before the laughter cleared, Dixon noticed Bertrand becoming aware of those eyes and looking away. Disturbed by this feeling of strain in the company, and finding now that Gore-Urquhart's eyes were fixed on him,

Dixon touched his glasses on to the right part of his nose and said, for something to say: 'Well, it's an unexpected pleasure to be drinking pints at one of these occasions.'

'You're in luck, Dixon,' Gore-Urquhart said sharply, passing round cigarettes.

Dixon felt himself going rather red, and decided to say no more for a time. But he was pleased that Gore-Urquhart had caught his name. With a loud braying noise, the music started again in the Ballroom and people began to move out of the bar. Bertrand, who'd settled himself next to Gore-Urquhart, began talking to him in a low voice, and almost at once Christine made some remark to Carol. Margaret said to Dixon: 'It is sweet of you to have brought me here, James.'

'Glad you're enjoying yourself.'

'You don't sound as if you are very much.'

'Oh, I am, really.'

'I'm sure you're enjoying this part of it better than the actual dancing part.'

'Oh, I'm enjoying both parts, honestly. Drink that up and we'll go back on the floor. I can do this kind of dance.'

She looked earnestly at him and rested a hand on his arm. 'Dear James, do you think it's wise for us to go round together like this?' she asked him.

'Why on earth not?'

'Because you're so sweet to me and I'm getting much too fond of you.' She said this in the voice she always used for such confessions, like a great actress showing how to express strong emotion in controlled tones.

Even in the panic this caused him, Dixon managed to find the thought that this, if true, would indeed be a reason for their seeing less of each other; then he hit on

C

a remark both honest and pleasing: 'You mustn't say things like that.'

She laughed lightly. 'Poor James,' she said.

He began to listen to the conversation on his left. Bertrand, almost talking instead of baying, was boasting shamelessly, and yet the Gore-Itchbag fellow, not apparently brainless, was listening to this outpouring of self-advertisement without open protest, even with some attention. Yes, Dixon saw, with very close attention. Gore-Urquhart was leaning towards Bertrand, his eyes on the floor, as if he couldn't bear to miss a word. Dixon couldn't bear not to miss any more of it. It was Margaret who broke in. 'Now, Mr Gore-Urquhart, I'm not going to allow any more of this sitting about in here, whether the Principal catches you or not. It's the dance-floor for you; come on.'

Gore-Urquhart, smiling politely, had risen to his feet and, with a word to the others, let himself be led away out of the bar. Bertrand looked across at Carol. 'Don't let's waste the band, my dear,' he said. 'I've paid twenty-five shillings for them.'

'So you have, my dear,' Carol said, putting extra weight into the 'my dear', and for a moment Dixon was afraid she meant to refuse and so cause the situation, whatever it was, to explode, but after that moment she got to her feet and began to move towards the dance-floor.

'Look after Christine for me, Dixon,' Bertrand bayed. 'Don't drop her; she's breakable. Good-bye for a little, my sweet,' he sang to Christine, 'I'll be back soon. Blow your whistle if the man gets rough.'

'Would you like to dance?' Dixon said to Christine. 'I'm not much good, as I told you, but I don't mind trying, if you don't.'

She smiled. 'Nor do I, if you don't.'

CHAPTER 10

As he left the bar with Christine at his side, Dixon kept careful control over his face to stop it doing what it wanted to do and breaking out into an imbecile grin of excitement and pride. When she turned and faced him at the edge of the floor, he found it hard to believe that she was really going to let him touch her, or that the men near them wouldn't immediately interfere to prevent him. But in a moment they were actually dancing together, not very skilfully, but without doubt dancing. There were a good many more people on the floor than a quarter of an hour earlier. Among the dancers he recognised Barclay, the Professor of Music, dancing with his wife. She permanently resembled a horse, he only when he laughed, which he did suddenly and seldom, but was momentarily to be seen doing now.

'What was the matter with Mrs Goldsmith, do you know?' Christine asked.

This curiosity surprised him. 'She did look rather unhappy, didn't she?' he said, to avoid answering.

'Was it because she was expecting Bertrand to bring her here tonight instead of me?'

Did that mean she knew about the switch of partners? It needn't, but it might. 'I don't know,' he said, keeping the expression out of his voice.

'I think you do know.' She sounded quite angry. 'I wish you'd tell me.'

'I know nothing at all about it, I'm afraid. And in any case it's nothing to do with me.'

'If that's the way you look at it, then there's nothing more to be said.'

61

Dixon felt himself going red for the second time in the last few minutes. Obviously she'd been most natural when helping Bertrand to annoy him when they first met, when scolding him for drinking too much, when treating him this evening as if he didn't exist. Her formal, not her easy, attitude was the true one. Her cheerful help with the sheet had been given in return for story-material likely to amuse her London acquaintances; her friendliness over the telephone had been to get something from him. No doubt she was disturbed by the Bertrand–Carol business, but the female trick of working off displeasure on any man who was at hand was one he'd learnt to recognise and dislike.

They danced in silence for some time. She'd not been modest in saying she was a poor dancer, but Dixon's necessary avoidance of anything ambitious kept them fairly well together. Everybody else on the floor seemed to be talking, and presently a female voice rather like Christine's, heard close by, deceived Dixon. 'What did you say?' he asked.

'Nothing.'

Something would have to be said by him now, so he said what he'd been waiting to say all the evening. 'I never got a chance to say thank you for supporting me so well over that telephone business.'

'What telephone business?'

'You know, me pretending to Bertrand that I was a reporter.'

'Oh that. I'd rather not discuss that, if you don't mind.'

She couldn't be allowed to dismiss it like that. 'Supposing I do mind?'

'What do you mean?'

'You seem to forget that if I hadn't made that little pretence you probably wouldn't be here at all tonight.'

'Well, that wouldn't have mattered very much, would it?'

The dance came to an end, but neither of them thought of leaving the floor. Through the applause he said: 'No, perhaps it wouldn't, but you seemed to want to come at that time, didn't you?'

'Look, can't you stop talking about it?'

'All right, but don't you try to play the queen over me. You've no reason to do that.'

She dropped her eyes. 'I'm sorry; that was silly of me. I didn't mean to be like that.'

As she spoke, a tinkling piano introduction led into the last dance of the set. 'All right, then,' Dixon said. 'Dance?'

'Yes, of course.'

They moved off again. 'I think we're getting the swing of this quite well,' he said in a moment.

'I wish I hadn't said what I did. I was a fool. I acted like a complete fool.'

He saw that when, as now, she abandoned her fixed expression, her lips were full and generous like her uncle's. 'It's all right, really, it was nothing,' he said.

'No, it wasn't nothing; it was ridiculous. I thought the whole of the *Evening Post* business was brilliantly funny.'

'Oh, come, there's no need to go to the opposite extreme.'

'But, you see, I didn't feel like discussing it with you because that would have been like laughing at Bertrand behind his back, and that would have been wrong.'

In the bar again, they found Gore-Urquhart in his former chair, already being talked to by Bertrand, as if their conversation had never been interrupted. Margaret was paying very close attention. She stopped laughing at one of Gore-Urquhart's quick answers to give Dixon a careless look which suggested that she was wondering

without much interest who he might be. More drinks
arrived—double gins. They were brought, of course, by
Maconochie, one of whose duties on these occasions was
to prevent the drinking of spirits. Dixon, who was
beginning to do what he'd have described as 'feeling his
age', sat down in a chair and began drinking his drink and
smoking a cigarette. How hot it was; and how his legs
ached; and how much longer was all this going to go on?
After a moment he told himself he must talk to Christine,
but she was sitting next to Bertrand and, though he was
taking no notice of her, was evidently listening to what he
was saying to her uncle, who was keeping his eyes on the
floor in the way that Dixon had observed earlier. Margaret
was laughing again, swaying towards Gore-Urquhart so
that their shoulders kept touching. Oh well, Dixon thought,
each must enjoy himself as and when he can. But where
was Carol?

Just then she reappeared, walking towards them with a
kind of deliberate carelessness that made Dixon suspect
her of having a bottle of something, now no doubt nearly
empty, hidden in the ladies' room. The expression on her
face held a threat for somebody, or perhaps everybody.
When she reached the group, Dixon saw Gore-Urquhart
look up at her and try to flash some signal; 'You see how
I am caught' was what his face seemed to say. Then he
stood up.

Carol turned to Dixon. 'Come on, Jim,' she said rather
loudly, 'I want you to dance with me. I suppose that
nobody here will object.'

CHAPTER 11

'What's the matter, Carol?'

'That's what I'd like to know.'

'What do you mean?'

'You know what I mean, Jim, unless you go about with your eyes shut. And you don't do that, do you? No, I'm sick and tired of being pushed around. I don't mind telling you this, because I know you. I do know you, don't I? What are you going to do about it, in any case?'

'About what?'

'What are you doing about Christine Callaghan?'

'Nothing, of course. What can I do?'

'If you don't know what to do, I can't show you. Are you worried about what dear Margaret would do?'

'Do stop this, Carol. You're supposed to be telling me something, not questioning me.'

'Don't worry; it's all connected, all connected. No, you leave Margaret to worry about her own troubles. I've met people like that before, old boy, and believe me, it's the only way, only thing to do. Throw a lifebelt and she'll pull you under. That's a fact.' She nodded, her eyes half-closed. 'Please, Jim, can't we go and sit down for a minute or two? This is too much like an Autumn sale for me.'

'All right.'

They made their way with difficulty to two chairs against the wall. As soon as they were seated, Carol leaned over to Dixon. 'I suppose you've guessed what has been going on between me and our friend the painter, haven't you? The only thing to settle now is what you're going to do about Christine, Jim.'

'I've told you: nothing.'

'Put dear Margaret out of your mind for a change.'

'It's nothing to do with her. It's just that I . . . well, I don't want to try to start anything with Christine, that's all.'

'I've heard that story before, but it's a good one. I always laugh at that one.'

'No, honestly, Carol. I'd much rather see her once or twice and not do anything about it—what could I do about it in any case? She's a bit out of my class, don't you think? If I did try to do anything I'd only get a slap in the face. We're both tied up with other . . .'

'You sound as if you're in love with her.'

'Do you think so?' he said, almost eagerly. He couldn't help regarding her remark as a compliment—one that he'd been needing for a long time, too.

'In any case, you've got a moral duty,' Carol said. 'Get that girl away from Bertrand; she wouldn't enjoy an affair with him. It wouldn't be her kind of thing at all. Mind you remember that.'

They re-entered the bar. Dixon felt that he'd been doing this for weeks. The sight of their party still, or again, just where they'd been before made him want very much to fall forward on to the floor and go to sleep. Bertrand was talking; Gore-Urquhart was listening; Margaret was laughing, but now she had a hand on Gore-Urquhart's nearest shoulder. She had taken off her glasses, a sure sign that she was allowing herself to enjoy life. Christine, her back to Dixon, was sitting as still as if she'd been turned into stone. A sudden burst of terror showered itself all over Dixon. After a moment he realised that this was because he had made a plan and was about to carry it out. He panted a little with the wickedness of it, then sat down in an empty chair next to Christine, who turned to him with a smile; rather an unhappy smile, he thought. 'Oh, hullo,' she said.

'Will you come? I am ordering the taxi in any case.'

'You look as if you're being rather left out of things here,' Dixon said.

'Yes, Bertrand's always the same when he starts talking like this. But I mean, of course he did really come here to meet Uncle.'

'I can see that.' Just at that moment Bertrand got up from his seat and, without looking in Christine's direction, walked across to where Carol was. A faint bay of greeting could be heard. Glancing at Christine, Dixon saw her actually in the process of blushing. He said quickly: 'Now listen to me, Christine. I'm going to go out and order a taxi now. It should be here in about a quarter of an hour. You come outside then and I'll take you back to the Welches' in it. There'll be no tricks; I promise that. Straight home to the Welches'.'

Her immediate reaction looked like anger. 'Why? Why should I?'

'Because you're fed up, and no wonder. That's why.'

'That's nothing to do with it. It's a ridiculous idea. Absolutely mad.'

'Will you come? I'm ordering the taxi in any case.'

'Don't ask me that. I don't want to be asked that.'

'But I am asking you. What do you say? I'll give you twenty minutes to decide.' He looked her in the eyes and laid his hand on her elbow. He must be mad to be talking to a girl like this like this. 'Please come,' he said.

She snatched her arm away. 'Oh don't,' she said, as if he'd been telling her that she had to have a tooth pulled out in the morning.

'I'll wait for you,' he said in a low urgent tone. 'At the entrance. Twenty minutes. Don't forget.'

He turned and left by a route that gave a view of part of the dance-floor and the band. She wouldn't come, of course, but at least he'd made his gesture. In other words, he'd thought of a way of hurting himself more severely than usual, and in public. He stopped for a moment to wave good-bye to the band, then receiving no answering waves, went to find a telephone.

Dixon paused at the entrance to light the cigarette which, according to his rules, he ought to be lighting after breakfast on the next day but one. The taxi he'd ordered was due at any time now. If by the time he'd finished his cigarette Christine had still not appeared, he'd just ask the taximan to take him to his lodgings, so whatever happened he'd be in a car soon. That was good, because very soon he would be quite unable to move.

After about twenty-five minutes his second cigarette was finished, and he not only had no Christine but no taxi. At that moment a car came round the corner from the main road and stopped near him. It was a taxi. A voice from the driver's seat said: 'Barker?'

'What do you mean, barker?'

'Taxi for Barker.'

'Barker? Oh, you must mean Barclay, don't you?'

'Yes, that's it: Barclay.'

'Good. We're nearly ready now. Just back round that corner, will you? and I'll be out in a couple of minutes. I may be taking a friend back with me. Don't let anyone else hire you. I'll be coming back.'

'That'll be all right, Mr. Barclay.'

Dixon walked briskly back and looked up the lighted passage, wondering whether he dared go and try Christine again. A bend hid all but the first few yards of the passage from his view. Without delay Professor Barclay appeared round this bend, struggling into his overcoat and followed by his wife. Dixon had a feeling that he had heard him mentioned recently in some connection.

The Barclays stood for a minute or two at the entrance, while nobody came and nobody went. Dixon glanced desperately up the passage. Two people appeared round the bend in it almost together. The first one wasn't Christine, but a drunk man madly trying to make a cigarette-lighter work. But the second one was.

The way she came was so ordinary that Dixon was almost shaken. He didn't know what he'd expected, but it wasn't this look of recognition on her face, this purposeful walk towards him. Glancing over at the line of cars outside, she said at once: 'Did you manage to get one?'

Dixon knew that the Barclays, or Mrs Barclay at least, would be listening. He hesitated for a second, then said 'Yes' and patted his pocket. 'I've got it here.'

He tried to get her to walk away with him, but she stayed where she was in the entrance, the lights from the passage leaving her face in shadow. 'I meant a taxi.'

'A taxi? A taxi? Just for three or four hundred yards?' He gave a disbelieving laugh. 'I'll have you back with Mother in less time than it'd take to telephone. Good night, Professor; good night, Mrs Barclay. Well it's fortunate we haven't got far to go. Did you say good-bye to the others for me?' They were far enough away by now for him to add: 'Good. That's fine. Well done.' Behind him he heard Mrs Barclay say something to her husband.

'What's happening?' Christine asked without attempting to hide her curiosity. 'What's all this about?'

'We've pinched their taxi; that's one of the things that's happening. It's waiting just round this corner.'

He got in beside Christine and the car started.

CHAPTER 12

'That was all very efficient,' Christine said. 'You're getting good at this sort of thing, aren't you? First the table, then the *Evening Post* thing, and now this.'

'I used not to be. I hope you don't object too much to the way I got hold of this taxi.'

'I've got into it, haven't I?'

'Did you manage to get away all right?' he asked.

'Oh yes; nobody seemed to mind very much.'

'What did you say to them?'

'I just explained things to Uncle Julius—he never minds what I do—and then I just told Bertrand I was going.'

'How did he react to that?'

'He said, "Oh, don't do that, I'll be with you in a minute." Then he went on talking to Mrs Goldsmith and Uncle. So I came away then.'

'I see. It all sounds very easy and quick.'

'Oh, it was.'

'Well, I'm very glad you decided to come with me after all.'

'Good. I couldn't help feeling rather guilty, at first, about walking out and leaving them all, but that feeling's gone now.'

'Good. What finally made you make up your mind?'

After a silence, she said: 'I wasn't enjoying it very much in there, as you know, and I started feeling very tired, and it didn't look as if Bertrand could leave for some time, so I thought I'd come with you.'

She said this in her best schoolmistressy way, elocution-mistressy, in fact, so Dixon repeated as stiffly: 'I see.' In

71

the light of a street-lamp he could see her sitting, as he'd expected, right on the edge of the seat.

She suddenly spoke again in her other manner, the one he associated with their telephone conversation: 'No, I'm not going to try and pretend that was it. That's only a part of it. I don't see why I shouldn't tell you a bit more. I left because I was feeling absolutely fed up with everything.'

'A girl like you's no reason to be fed up with everything, Christine,' Dixon said warmly. 'I'd have thought of you as somebody reasonably successful in most things.'

'I didn't mean to sound like a martyr. You're right, of course, I do have a good time and I've been very lucky in all sorts of ways. But, you know, I do find some things extremely difficult. I don't really know the right things to do, you know.'

Dixon wanted to laugh. He couldn't imagine a woman of her age less in need of such knowledge. He said so.

'No, it's quite true,' she insisted. 'I haven't had a chance to find out yet.'

'You mustn't mind my saying this, but I should have thought there'd be plenty of people only too willing to show you.'

'I know. I see what you mean exactly. But they don't try to. They assume I know already, you see.' She was talking eagerly now.

'Oh, they do, do they? Why is that, do you think?'

'I think it must be because I look as if I'm full of poise and that sort of thing. Two or three people have told me that, so it must be right. But it's only that I look like that.'

'Yes, I suppose it is. But it isn't just that alone, is it?'

'Sorry: what isn't what alone?'

'I mean it's not just your appearance that makes you

seem older and more experienced and so on. It's the way you behave and talk, a lot of the time, too. Don't you think so?'

'Well, it's very hard for me to tell, isn't it?'

'It must be, naturally. It's . . . you seem to . . . keep getting on to your high horse all the time; hard to describe it exactly. But you've got a habit, now and then, of talking and behaving like a schoolmistress.'

'Oh, have I?'

Although the tone of this question illustrated just what he was talking about, Dixon, feeling it couldn't matter what he said, said: 'There, you're doing it now. When you don't know what to do or say, you defend yourself by becoming starchy. And that all fits in with your face; that's probably what gave you the idea of being starchy to begin with, your face, I mean. And that makes a total effect of a rather priggish kind of self-confidence, and you don't want to be priggish but you do want to be self-confident. Yes. . . . But that's quite enough of Uncle Jim's Corner for Young Readers. We're getting away from the point. What has all this to do with being fed up? There's still nothing to be fed up about.'

She hesitated while Dixon sweated slightly, then she said with a rush: 'When I met Bertrand he didn't seem to be quite like the other men I have met, chiefly because he didn't start trying to make love to me all the time. And he can be very nice, you know, though I don't suppose you . . . After a time I was starting to get rather fond of him, and at the same time—this is the funny part—I was getting a bit fed up with him in other ways while I was still getting more fond of him. He's such a queer mixture, you see.'

Naming to himself the two substances of which he

personally thought Bertrand a mixture, Dixon said: 'In what way?'

'He can be extremely understanding and kind one minute, and completely unreasonable and childish the next. I feel I never know where I am with him, or what he really wants. Sometimes I think it's all to do with how he's getting along with his painting. Anyhow, for one reason or another we started having rows. And I can't bear rows, especially because he was always putting me in the wrong by them.'

'How do you mean?'

'You know, he'd start one with me when he could put me in the wrong by starting one, and force me to start one when starting one would put whoever started one in the wrong. There'll be one about tonight, of course, and he'll put me in the wrong as usual. But he's in the wrong; he's the one that's wrong. All this business with Mrs Goldsmith—it's all right, I'm not going to ask you about it— but I know there's something happening, but he won't tell me what it is. I don't suppose it's serious; he just gets a bit excited when . . . But he won't tell me what's happening. He'll pretend there isn't anything, and he'll ask me if I really think he'd do anything behind my back, and I'll have to say No, otherwise . . .'

'It's not my business, Christine, but in my opinion friend Bertrand's qualifying for good-bye from you.'

'No, I . . . Jim,' Christine said.

Dixon sat up sharply at this, the first use of his christian name. 'Yes?' he said, ready to face an attack.

'You've been very kind to me tonight. And you seem to have a lot of common sense. Would you mind if I asked your advice on something?'

'No, not at all.'

'You must realise, though, that I'm asking you just because I want to hear your advice, not for any other reason.' She paused, then added: 'You understand that?'

'Yes, of course.'

'Well, it's this. From what you've seen of both of us, do you think it would be a good thing if I got married to Bertrand?'

Dixon could not quite explain to himself the unpleasant taste that came to his mouth. 'Isn't that rather your affair?'

'Of course it's my affair; I'm the one who's going to marry him or not marry him. I want to know what you think. I'm not asking to be told what to do. Now what do you think?'

This was clearly the moment for a burst of accurate shelling from Dixon in his Bertrand-war, but he found himself not quite willing to fire. A reasoned attack on his enemy's character, followed by a short account of the Carol affair, would have a good chance of bringing total victory, or at least of causing heavy losses. But he felt that he didn't want to do it like that, and only said slowly: 'I don't think I know either of you well enough.'

'Ah, hell, man'—had she learnt that from Uncle Julius? Dixon wondered—'you're not being asked to write a learned book about it. What do you think?'

'Well, it's . . . I must say what I think, you know.'

'Yes, yes, of course. That's what I asked for, isn't it?'

'Well then, I should say No.'

'I see. Why not?'

'Because I like you and I don't like him.'

'Is that all?'

'It's quite enough. It means each of you belongs to one

of the two great classes of mankind, people I like and
people I don't.'

A movement of Christine's, the first he'd noticed since
the journey began, made him glance in her direction. He
could see that she was leaning forward and looking out of
the window. He heard her yawn. 'Where are we now, do
you think?'

'Oh, just over half-way, I should think.'

'I feel very sleepy. I don't want to be sleepy.'

'Have a cigarette. That'll help you.'

'No thanks. I say, would you mind if I shut my eyes
for a few minutes? It'll make me feel much less tired, I
know.'

'Of course. Go to sleep.'

While she curled herself up in her corner, Dixon fought
his disappointment at this trick of hers for escaping from
his company. He'd thought he was making such good progress. Just then she laid her head on his shoulder and all
his senses grew alert. 'You don't mind, do you?' she
asked. 'The back of the seat's like iron.'

'Of course you can.' Forcing himself to act before he
could think, he slid his arm beneath her shoulders. She
moved her head experimentally to and fro against him,
then settled herself and seemed to go to sleep at once.

Dixon's heart began to beat rather fast. He now had
all the evidence he wanted that she was there: he was
aware of her breathing; the top of her head against his
jaw and her shoulder under his hand were warm; her
hair smelt of well-brushed hair; he could feel the presence
of her body. It was a pity it wasn't accompanied by the
presence of her mind.

The taxi swung round a bend and he braced himself
with his foot to hold his position and hers. He couldn't

go to sleep himself, but he could make sure that she stayed asleep.

With great care he moved a little closer to Christine.

Presently the driver slid the glass aside and asked for more instructions, which Dixon gave. At last the taxi stopped at the end of the track that led up to the Welch house. Christine woke up and said after a moment: 'Are you coming up? I hope you will, because I'm not quite sure how I'm going to get in. The maid lives at home, I think.'

'Of course I'll come up,' Dixon said. He settled a brief argument with the taxi-driver by refusing to discuss the question of payment until the taxi should be standing outside his, Dixon's lodgings, then went off into the darkness with Christine holding on to his arm.

CHAPTER 13

'I think we'd better look for a window first,' Dixon said as they stood in front of the darkened house. 'We don't want to ring the bell, just in case the Welches have got back before us. I don't suppose they'd want to be home very late.'

'Wouldn't they have to wait for Bertrand, because of the car?'

'They might have got a taxi; anyhow, I'm not ringing that bell.'

They went off carefully into the yard at the left side of the building. In the darkness Dixon came against something which struck him skilfully on the shin and made him swear in a whisper.

Christine laughed in a muffled way, as if her hands were over her mouth. By touch, and the sight which the minutes in the dark had given him, Dixon discovered that the object was a water-tap enclosed in wood which was split and half-wrecked by some recent blow, as of a badly driven car. He hummed a little of his Welch tune, then said to Christine: 'That's enough, that's enough. This looks like the sitting-room window; we'll just try that in case.'

'Is it open?' Christine asked at his elbow. In whisper her voice had the same very young quality he'd noticed on the telephone.

'Yes, it seems to be.' He pulled the window slowly open and stepped into the room past the long curtain. All the other curtains were apparently drawn and the room was like a closed box. He moved slowly forward, his arms stretched out, until some piece of furniture struck him the pair to the blow he'd just received. There was an extraordinary moment when he and Christine reacted exactly as before. His hands felt their way round two walls until he found the light-switch. 'I'm going to put the light on,' he said. 'All right?'

'Yes.'

'Right.' He snapped the switch down and by instinct turned away from it as the room sprang into light around them. His movement brought him very close to Christine. They looked at each other, both blinking and smiling; their faces were about on a level. Then the smile left her face and was replaced by a look that suggested anxiety. Her eyes were narrowed; her mouth moved silently; she seemed to raise her arms. Dixon took the step that separated them, and then, very slowly at first to give her all the time she might need to step back and away, put his arms round her. She was breathing in when he finally took his grasp and so at this she caught her breath. He kissed her for some seconds, not holding her too close; her lips were dry, and hard rather than soft; she felt very warm. At last she did step back. She looked an unlikely figure under the bright light; she might have been an effect of trick photography. Dixon felt as if he'd been running for a bus and had been knocked over by a car at the same time. He could only say: 'Well, that was very nice,' with a sort of wooden liveliness.

'Yes, wasn't it?'

'Worth coming back from the dance for.'

'Yes.' She turned away. 'Oh look, we're in luck. I wonder who thought of this.'

A tray with cups, a flask, and biscuits stood on a small round table. Dixon, who'd been feeling inclined to tremble, found his spirits going up like a bird at the sight; it meant he wouldn't have to leave for at least a quarter of an hour. 'Very kind of somebody,' he said.

In a minute they were sitting side by side. 'I think you'd better drink out of my cup,' Christine said. 'We don't want anyone to know you've been here, do we?' She poured out some coffee and drank a little, then passed the cup to him.

Dixon felt that this sharing of the cup somehow represented and crowned the whole evening. 'I'm very fond of you,' he said.

He caught a glimpse of the starchier manner as she replied: 'How can you be? You hardly know me.'

'I know enough to be sure of that, thanks. Tell me: how long are you staying here this time?

'For a few days. It's part of my holiday.'

'Excellent. When can you come out with me?'

'Oh, don't be such a fool, Jim. How can I possibly come
out with you?'

'No difficulty at all, Christine. You can pretend you're
out with Uncle Julius. From what I've seen of him I'm
sure he'd support your story.'

'Don't say any more. We're both tied up.'

'We can start worrying about that, if we've got to, when
we've seen a little more of each other.'

'Do you realise what you're asking me to do? I'm a
guest at this place, Bertrand asked me to come, and I'm
his . . . I'm tied up with him. Can't you see yourself how
unfair it would be?'

'No, because I don't like Bertrand.'

'That doesn't make any difference.'

'Yes, it does. I don't say "After you, old boy" to fellows
like him.'

'Well, what about Margaret, then?'

'You've got a point there, Christine. But she's got no
real claim on me, you know.'

'Hasn't she? She seems to think she has.'

When Dixon hesitated, he was aware of the complete
silence. He turned in his seat, so that he was directly facing
her, and said in a softer tone. 'Look, Christine, let's see it
this way. Would you like to come out with me? Forgetting
about Bertrand and Margaret for the moment.'

'You know I would,' she said at once. 'Why do you think
I let you take me away from the dance?'

'So you did . . .' He looked at her, and she looked back
with her chin lifted and her mouth not quite closed. He
put an arm round her shoulders and bent towards the
neat blonde head. They kissed more earnestly than before.

Dixon felt as if he were being drawn downwards into some dark region where the air was too heavy to breathe with comfort and the blood became thin and slow. When she moved again he let her go. She smiled at him in a way that made him dizzier than the kiss had done.

When he didn't speak, she said, 'Yes, all right, then, but I still think it's not fair. What do you suggest?'

Dixon felt like a man interrupted at the moment he is receiving the Order of Merit to be told that a six-figure cheque from a football pool is waiting for him downstairs. 'There's a very nice hotel in the town where we could have dinner,' he said.

'No, I don't think we'd better arrange anything for an evening, if you don't mind.'

'All right, then. What about a tea?'

'Yes, a tea'd be splendid. Tuesday?'

'Excellent. Four o'clock?' He explained how to get to the hotel where they were to meet, and had hardly finished when they heard unmistakable and growing sounds of a car. 'Here they are,' he said, whispering again by instinct.

'What are you going to do?'

'I'll wait until they've started coming in the front door, and then slip out by the window. You close it behind me.'

'Right.'

The car began moving along the front of the house. 'You're quite clear about where to meet?' he asked.

'Don't you worry. I'll be there. Four o'clock.'

They went over to the window and stood there with their arms round each other while the car's engine, after a terrible rattling roar, died away.

'Thanks for a lovely evening, Christine.'

'Good night, Jim.' She pressed herself to him and they kissed for a moment, then she pushed him towards the window, which they reached just as Welch's voice, in its high-pitched madman's tone, came to their ears from the passage. 'Quick. See you on Tuesday. Good night.'

CHAPTER 14

Dixon had to write up some of his notes for the Merrie England lecture. But before that he must review his financial position, see if he could somehow restore it from complete impossibility to its usual level of merely imminent disaster, and before that again he must think, just for a couple of minutes, about the unbelievable ending to the Summer Ball the previous evening and about Christine.

He found himself unable to think effectively about, hardly even to remember, what they'd said to each other at the Welches', nor could he now recall what it had been like kissing her more clearly than that he'd enjoyed it. He was already so excited about Tuesday afternoon that he had to get up and walk about in his room. The important thing was to convince himself that she wouldn't come; then whatever happened would be something extra. The trouble was that he could imagine exactly how she'd look coming across the hotel lounge towards him. Then he found he could see her face quite clearly in his mind.

He was just getting out his Merrie England notes when there was a knock at his door and Margaret came in. She was wearing the green Paisley dress and the velvet shoes.

'Hullo, Margaret,' he said with a heartiness which came, he realised, from a guilty conscience. But why had he got a guilty conscience. Leaving her with Gore-Urquhart

'Do you hate me, James?'

at the Ball had been doing the 'right thing', hadn't it?

She looked at him with her expression which suggested doubt about who he was, an expression which had often, without any other aid, beaten him to the ground. 'Oh, hullo,' she said. Still looking at him, she shook her head slowly, like a doctor letting it be known that there is no hope. Her face looked yellowish, and her nose seemed pinched. 'Do you hate me, James?'

Dixon wanted to rush at her and push her backwards, to make a deafening rude noise in her face, to push a bead up her nose. 'What do you mean?' he asked.

It took her a quarter of an hour to make clear what she meant. She talked fast, her head jerking to replace hair she imagined to have come loose, her thumbs bending and straightening. Why had he deserted her at the Ball like that? or rather, since she and he and everyone else knew why, what was he trying to do? or rather, again, how could he do this to her? In exchange for such information on these and other problems as he could give, she offered the news that all three Welches were 'out for his blood' and that Christine had made a remark showing a low opinion of him at breakfast that morning. No mention of Gore-Urquhart was made except a passing attack on Dixon's 'rudeness' in leaving the dance without saying good night to him. Dixon knew from experience that to counter-attack Margaret was always a mistake, but he was too angry to consider that. When he was sure that she was going to say no more about Gore-Urquhart, he said, his heart beating rather fast: 'I don't see why you're making all this fuss. You looked as if you were looking after yourself all right when I left.'

'And what do you mean by that?'

'You were so interested in that Gore-Itchbag fellow you

hadn't got time to say a single word to me, had you? If you didn't succeed in interesting him, it wasn't for the lack of trying. I've never seen such a display in my life. . . .' His voice faded into silence; he couldn't manufacture enough of the necessary indignation.

She stared at him wide-eyed. 'But you can't mean . . . ? '

'Oh yes I can; of course I can mean.'

'James . . . you don't know . . . what you're talking about,' she said slowly and painfully, like a foreigner reading out of a phrase-book. 'Really, I'm so surprised; I just . . . don't know what to say.' She began to tremble. 'I talk to a man, just for a few minutes, that's all it was . . . and now you start accusing me of trying to win him. That's what you mean. Isn't that what you mean? ' There was an ugly shaking in her voice.

He remembered Carol's phrase about not throwing Margaret any lifebelts. Well, he'd thrown his last one. 'Look here, Margaret,' he said, 'I've no desire to hurt your feelings unnecessarily, as you know perfectly well. But for your own sake, as well as mine, you must understand something clearly. I know you've had a very hard time recently, and you know I know that as well. But it won't do you any good to go on thinking what you evidently do think about me and the relations between us. It'll only make things worse. What I want to say is, you must stop depending on me emotionally like this. I agree I was probably in the wrong over the dance business, but right or wrong won't make any difference to this. I'll be on your side and I'll talk to you and I'll sympathise, but I've had enough of being forced into a false position. I am not in love with you.'

There was a pause; then she came blindly and unsteadily forward; put her hands on his shoulders, and seemed to

collapse on to the bed. Her glasses fell off and she made
no move to save them. She was making a curious noise, a
steady, repeated, low moan that sounded as if it came from
far down in her stomach, as if she'd been sick again and
again and still wanted to be sick. Then she raised herself,
stiff but still trembling, and began a series of high-pitched
screams thrown in between the deep moans. Both were
quite loud. Her hair was in her eyes, her lips were drawn
back, and her face was wet, from her mouth as well as her
eyes. Suddenly she screamed half a dozen times, very
loudly, then went on more quietly, moaning with every
outward breath. Two sets of footsteps were now approaching outside, one coming up and the other down the stairs.
The door opened and Bill Atkinson came in, followed by
the lady of the house, Miss Cutler. Dixon looked up at
them.

'Hysterics, eh?' Atkinson said, and slapped Margaret
several times on the face, very hard, Dixon thought. He
pushed Dixon out of the way, and sat down on the bed,
gripping Margaret by the shoulders and shaking her hard.
'There's some whisky up in my cupboard. Go and get it.'

Dixon ran out and up the stairs. The only thought that
came to him at all clearly was one of mild surprise that
the treatment of hysterics in stories and films should be
what was evidently the right treatment. He found the
whisky. His hand was shaking so much that he nearly
dropped the bottle. He uncorked it and took a quick
swallow, trying not to cough. Down in his room again, he
found everything much quieter. Miss Cutler, who'd been
watching Atkinson and Margaret, gave Dixon a glance,
not of suspicion or blame, but of reassurance; she said
nothing. As he felt at the moment, this made him want to
cry. Atkinson looked up without taking the bottle. 'Get a

glass or a cup.' He got a cup, poured some whisky into it, and gave it to Atkinson.

Atkinson pulled Margaret up into a half-sitting position. Her moans had stopped and she was trembling less violently. Her face was red from Atkinson's blows. When he put the cup to her mouth it rattled once or twice on her teeth and her breathing was loud. Then she coughed, swallowed, coughed again, swallowed some more. Quite soon she stopped trembling altogether and began to look round at them. 'Sorry about that,' she said faintly.

'That's all right, girlie,' Atkinson said. 'Like a smoke?'

'Yes, please.'

'Forward, Jim.'

Miss Cutler smiled at them all, appeared to say something, and went quietly out. Dixon lit cigarettes for the three of them and Margaret sat up on the edge of the bed; Atkinson still kept his arm round her. 'Were you the one that slapped my face?' she asked him.

'That's right, girlie. It did you a powerful amount of good. How do you feel now?'

'A lot better, thanks. A bit dizzy, but otherwise all right.'

'Good. Don't try to move about for a bit. Here, put your feet up and have a rest.'

'There's really no need . . .'

He pulled her feet up on to the bed and took off her shoes, then stood looking down at her. 'You stay here for ten minutes at least. I'll leave you to the care of brother Jim now. Have some more whisky when you've finished that, but don't let Jim get any. I promised his mother . . .' He turned to Dixon. 'All right, old man?'

'Yes, thanks, Bill. It's been very kind of you.'

'All right, girlie?'

'Thank you so much, Mr Atkinson; you've been wonder-ful. I just can't thank you enough.'

'That's all right, girlie.' He nodded to them and went out.

'I'm sorry about all that, James,' she said as soon as the door was shut.

'It was my fault.'

'No, you always say that. This time I'm not going to let you. I just couldn't take what you said, that's all. I thought to myself, I can't bear it, I must stop him, and then I simply lost control of myself. That's all it was. And it was all so silly and childish, because you were absolutely right, saying what you did. Much better to get everything clear like that. I just behaved like a complete fool.'

'There's no point in blaming yourself. You couldn't help it.'

After she'd gone, he began getting ready to work. He refused to think directly about Margaret's attack of hysterics. Soon enough, he knew, it would take its place with those three or four memories which could make him actually twist about in his chair or bed with regret, fear, or embarrassment.

CHAPTER 15

Dixon plunged down the lodging-house stairs at eight-fifteen the next morning because he wanted, or rather had got, to spend a long morning in preparing his Merrie

England lecture. He didn't like having breakfast so early. There was something about Miss Cutler's breakfasts which, bearable at nine o'clock, his usual breakfast-time, seemed at eight-fifteen to cause a revolution in every part of his body. He was alone in the room.

Avoiding thinking about Margaret, and for some reason not wanting to think about Christine, he found his thoughts turning towards his lecture. Early the previous evening he'd tried writing his notes for it up into a script. The first page of notes had produced a page and three lines of script. At that rate he'd be able to talk for eleven and a half minutes on the material at present in his notes. Something was evidently required for a further forty-eight and a half minutes, with perhaps a minute off for being introduced to the audience, another minute for water-drinking, coughing and page-turning, and nothing at all for applause. Where was he going to find extra material? The only answer to this question seemed to be Yes, that's right, where? Ah, wait a minute; he'd get Barclay to find him a book on medieval music. Twenty minutes at least on that, with an apology for 'having let my interest run away with me'. Welch would be delighted. He made faces at his coffee for a moment at the thought of having to copy down so many hateful facts, then cheered up at the thought of being able to do himself so much good without having to think at all. 'It may perhaps be thought,' he muttered to himself, 'that the character of an age, a nation, a class, would be but poorly revealed in anything so apparently distinct from ordinary habits of thought as its music, as its musical culture.' He leant forward over the table for impression. 'Nothing could be further from the truth.'

'I was wondering if you were doing anything this evening. I thought you might like to come and have a meal with us.'

After a day of doing Welch's work, there was plenty for Dixon to do that evening in connection with his lecture. He had been in search of material for it when Welch had caught him: 'I wonder if you would mind . . .' But it was obvious that he couldn't afford to refuse this offer, so he said unhesitatingly: 'Well, thank you very much, Professor. That's very kind of you.'

'Come along, then. We'll go in my car.'

'That'll be nice.'

Dixon's own thoughts and feelings, all the time they were getting into the car and driving off, were busy with the subject of Margaret. He didn't know how he was going to be able to meet her. He'd also have to meet Bertrand and Mrs Welch, he supposed, but these meetings must in comparison be less terrible. There'd be Christine as well; he didn't really want to see her either, not because of anything to do with her personality, but because she formed a part of his worry about Margaret. He'd have to do something to show Margaret she wasn't entirely alone; he wouldn't, he mustn't let himself, get back into the same relations with her, but he must somehow reassure her of his continued support. How was he going to do that?

The journey was uneventful. Welch's driving seemed to have improved slightly; at least, the only death Dixon felt himself threatened by was death from boredom. Welch talked all the time, his own face the perfect audience for his talk, laughing at its jokes, reflecting its puzzlement or earnestness, answering with tightened lips and narrowed eyes its more important points. He went on talking even while he drove up the sandy path into the yard next to his house, shaved the ruined water-tap, nosed into the garage entrance, and, with a single frightful leap, stopped the car a couple of inches from the wall on Dixon's side. Then he got out. It took Dixon some time to twist himself out of the trap and follow him.

As soon as Dixon joined the company inside the house, his quiet day jerked into mad activity. Welch swung round towards him; Christine, more apple-cheeked even than he remembered her, was grinning at him in the background; Mrs Welch and Bertrand moved in his direction; Margaret turned her back. Welch said with sudden energy: 'Oh, Faulkner.'

'Yes, Professor.'

'At least, Dixon.' He hesitated, then went on, speaking more clearly than Dixon had ever heard him: 'I'm afraid there's been a bit of a mix-up, Dixon. I'd forgotten that we'd all promised to go to the theatre this evening with the Goldsmiths. We shall have to have dinner early, so I shall just have time to change my clothes and drive us into town. There'll be room for you if you want a lift. I'm sorry about it, of course, but I shall have to rush off now. We must invite you another time.'

Before he was out of the room, Mrs Welch moved up to Dixon, Bertrand was at her side. Rather red in the face, she said: 'Oh, Mr Dixon, I've been wondering when I should see you again. I've one or two points I want to discuss with you. First of all, I'd like you to explain, if you can, what happened to the sheet and blankets on your bed when you were our guest here recently.' While Dixon was still trying to moisten his mouth enough to speak, she added: 'I'm waiting for an answer, Mr. Dixon.'

Dixon noticed that Christine and Margaret had moved away down the room together, talking quietly. 'I don't quite know what . . .' he mumbled. 'I didn't see . . .'

'Am I to understand that you deny having anything to do with it? If so, the only other person who might have done it is my maid, in which case I shall have to . . .'

'No,' Dixon interrupted, 'I don't deny it. Please, Mrs Welch, I'm extremely sorry about it all. I know I should have come to you and told you about it, but I'd done so much damage I was afraid to. It was silly, I know. Will you send me the bill for what it costs you to replace the sheet and blankets?' Thank heaven they still didn't know about the table.

'Of course, Mr Dixon, you will get the bill. But I want to hear how the damage was caused. Exactly what happened, please?'

'I know I've behaved very badly, Mrs Welch, but please don't ask me to explain that. I've apologised and promised to pay for the damage; won't you let me keep the explanation to myself? It's nothing very terrible, I can assure you of that.'

'Then why do you refuse to say what it is?'

'I don't refuse; I am only asking you not to cause me a lot of embarrassment that wouldn't help you at all.'

Bertrand now joined in. Putting his untidy face over to one side, he brought it nearer, saying: 'We can bear that, Dixon. It won't hurt us to bear your embarrassment. It'll be some kind of small return for the way you've behaved.'

Mrs Welch turned away. 'I think I'll just go and see if your father's nearly ready, darling,' she said. 'There are one or two things I want him to . . .' Leaving the sentence in the air, she went out.

Bertrand moved a step nearer. 'We'll forget all about that matter,' he said generously. 'Now I've been wanting us to have a little discussion for some time, old boy. Ever since that Ball affair, in fact. Now look here: here's a question for you, and I don't mind telling you I mean to get a direct answer. What exactly was your game when you persuaded Christine to slip away from the dance with you? A direct answer, now.'

Christine had come down the room with Margaret, and she must have heard this clearly. Both girls were careful not to look at Dixon while they went out, leaving him alone with Bertrand. When the door was shut, Dixon said: 'I can't give any sort of answer, direct or indirect, to a meaningless question. What do you mean, what was my game? I wasn't playing any sort of game.'

'You know what I mean as well as I do. What were you trying to do?'

'You'd better ask Christine that.'

'We'll leave her out of this, if you don't mind.'

'Why should I mind?' Dixon, in spite of the thought of how Mrs Welch's bill would swallow up his bank-balance, suddenly began to rejoice. The early moves for position were over; the real war between himself and Bertrand had started.

'Don't be funny, Dixon. Just tell me what the idea was, will you? or I shall have to try something a little more forceful.'

'Don't you be funny, either. What do you want to know?'

Bertrand clenched his fist; then, when Dixon took off his glasses and looked ready to fight, unclenched it again. Dixon put his glasses on again. 'I want to know . . .' Bertrand said, then hesitated.

'What my game was. We've discussed that.'

'Now just you get this into your head, Dixon. I've had enough of your funny little jokes. Christine is my girl and she stays my girl, understand?'

Dixon was saved from replying by the sudden re-entry
of Christine and Margaret. The scene broke up: Christine,
who seemed to be trying to flash Dixon a message he
couldn't read, took Bertrand by the arm and led him, still
loudly protesting, out of the room; Margaret silently
offered Dixon a cigarette, which he took. Neither spoke
while they sat down side by side, nor for some moments
afterwards. Dixon found himself trembling a good deal. He
looked at Margaret and an unbearable weight fell upon him.

He knew now what he'd been trying to conceal from
himself since the previous morning, what the row with
Bertrand had made him temporarily disbelieve: he and
Christine would not, after all, be able to eat tea together
the following afternoon. If he was going to eat that meal
with any female except Miss Cutler, it would be not
Christine, but Margaret.

'That was about the dance affair, was it?' Margaret
asked.

'Yes. He seemed to be rather angry about that.'

'I'm not surprised. What was he shouting?'

'He was trying to persuade me to keep off the grass.'

'As far as she's concerned?'

'That's right.'

'Are you going to?'

'Eh? What?'

'Are you going to keep off the grass?'

'Yes.'

'Why, James?'

'Because of you.'

He'd been expecting a show of some strong feeling, but
she only said, 'I think that's rather silly of you' in a
neutral tone that wasn't neutral for effect, but simply
neutral.

'What makes you say that?'

'I thought that was all settled yesterday. I don't see the point of starting the whole thing again.'

Dixon felt he was as usual not in control of the conversation. He said: 'Let's go to the pictures tonight. You needn't go to the theatre. Carol won't mind, I know.'

'I wasn't going, in any case.'

'That's all right, then.'

He reached out and took her hand: she made no movement. There was a pause, during which they heard someone run heavily downstairs into the hall. Margaret glanced at him for a moment, then turned her head away. In a dead sort of voice, she said: 'All right, I'll come to the pictures.'

'Good. I'll ask Neddy if we can go in the car. He can get six in. You go up and get ready.'

In the hall Margaret said: 'I shan't be a minute,' and went up the stairs. Dixon went out and stood on the step. At the sound of somebody else's step he turned and saw Christine coming towards him wearing a little black jacket, but otherwise dressed exactly as he'd seen her on the arty week-end. She smiled at him and joined him on the step. 'I hope you didn't have too bad a time with Bertrand,' she said.

'Bertrand? Oh . . . no, it was all right.'

'I managed to calm him down after a time.'

He watched her; she stood with her legs apart and looked very sturdy and confident. The breeze blew a little of the fair hair the wrong way. She half-closed her eyes as she faced the sun. It was as if she were about to do something dangerous, important, and simple which she knew she could make a good attempt at, whether she succeeded or not. A feeling of grief that was also a feeling of anger against fate settled upon Dixon. 'About this tea tomorrow,' he said.

'Yes?' she said, looking a little nervous. 'What about it?' As she said this, Welch started up his car at the side of the house. She added: 'You needn't worry. I'll be there all right.' Before he could reply she glanced over her shoulder into the hall and shook her finger at him, frowning.

Bertrand came out on to the step, glancing from one of them to the other. He was wearing a blue beret, which had the same effect on Dixon as the Professor's fishing-hat. If such headwear was a protection, what was it a protection against? If it wasn't a protection, what was it? What was it for?

As if guessing what he wanted to ask, Christine again frowned at him, then at Bertrand. 'Now, no matter what you two think of each other,' she said, 'please behave properly in front of Mr and Mrs Welch. I thought you'd both gone mad a few minutes ago.'

CHAPTER 16

Dixon realised with relief that the voice on the telephone at his lodgings was quite strange to him. It said: 'Oh, have you a Mr Dixon living there, please?'

'Speaking.'

'Oh, Mr Dixon, I'm so glad I've found you. Your University gave me the number. My name's Catchpole; I expect you've heard of me from Margaret Peel.'

Dixon grew tense. 'Yes, I have,' he said, with no special meaning in his tone. It wasn't the sort of voice he'd have expected Catchpole to have; it was quiet, polite, and apparently not very confident.

'I rang up because I thought you might be able to give some news of Margaret. I've been away recently, and I haven't managed to find out anything about her since I got back. How is she now, do you know?'

'Why don't you ring her up and ask her yourself? Or perhaps you've tried and she won't speak to you. Well, I can understand that.' Dixon was trembling now.

'I think there must be some mistake about . . .'

'I've got her address, but I don't see why I should give it to you—particularly you.'

'Mr Dixon, I can't understand why you're speaking to me like that. All I want to know is how Margaret is. There can't be anything wrong about that, can there?'

'I warn you that if you're thinking of getting back into favour, you're wasting your time, see?'

'I don't know what you mean by that. Are you sure you haven't got me confused with someone else?'

'Your name's Catchpole, isn't it?'

'Yes. Please . . .'

'Well, I know who you are, then. And I know all about you.'

'Please give me a hearing, Mr Dixon.' The voice at the other end shook slightly. 'I just wanted to know whether Margaret is all right or not. Won't you even tell me that?'

Dixon calmed down at this appeal. 'All right, I will. She's in quite good health physically. Mentally, she's about as well as can be expected.'

'Thanks very much. I'm glad to hear that. Do you mind if I ask you one more question?'

'What is it?'

'Why were you so angry with me a moment ago when I asked you about her?'

'That's obvious, isn't it?'

'Not to me, I'm afraid. I can't think of any reason why you should have a grudge against me. No real reason, that is.'

It sounded remarkably sincere. 'Well, I can,' Dixon said, unable to keep the puzzlement out of his voice.

'There's some kind of mix-up here, I can see that. I'd like to meet you some time, if I may, and try to clear things up. We can't do it over the telephone. Would you agree?'

Dixon hesitated. 'All right. What do you suggest?'

They arranged to meet for a pre-lunch drink in a pub at the foot of College Road the next day but one, Thursday. When Catchpole had rung off, Dixon sat for some minutes smoking. It was worrying, but then most of the things that had happened to him recently were that. Anyhow, he'd go to the pub and find out what it was about. Keep quiet about it to Margaret, of course.

Up in his room, Dixon got out the notes for his lecture and went on writing them up into a script.

Five hours later, he had what he estimated as forty-five minutes' worth of lecture. It seemed by then as if there were no facts anywhere in the world which could possibly be dragged in to fill the fifteen minutes still required. They would have to be occupied by an unusually long conclusion, and he didn't want to write one of those. Something like 'Finally, thank heaven for the twentieth century' would satisfy him, but it wouldn't satisfy Welch. Then he seized his pencil again, gave a happy laugh, and wrote: 'This survey, brief as it is, would have no purpose if left as a mere '—he crossed out 'mere '—'historical record. There are valuable lessons here for us, living in an age of ready-made amusements as we do. One wonders how one of the men or women I have tried to describe would react to such typical modern ideas as the cinema, the radio, the television. What would he think, accustomed as he was (had been? would have been? is?) to making his own music (must look at Welch at this point), of a society where people like himself are considered queer, where to play an instrument himself (oneself?) instead of paying others to do so, to . . .'

He stopped writing and ran into the bathroom. He started washing at his highest speed. He was just late enough; with luck he'd have time to get ready and rush along to the hotel for tea with Christine, but not time to think about tea with Christine. But in spite of all the energy of his movements, he began to feel very slightly sick at the thought of what was going to happen.

He arrived at the hotel two minutes late. On turning into the lounge where tea was served, he felt a sharp attack of fear, or whatever emotion it was, when he saw Christine already sitting waiting for him. He'd expected to have a few minutes in which to think of things to say to her; if it had been Margaret, he'd have had them and more.

She smiled as he approached. 'Hullo, Jim.'

He was feeling physically very nervous. 'Hullo,' he said with a half-cough. Fighting temptations to see that his tie was straight, his pockets tidy, his clothes properly buttoned, he sat down cautiously in front of her. Today she wore a jacket of the same material as her wine-coloured skirt, and these and the white blouse all seemed newly ironed. She looked so unmanningly pretty that Dixon's head began to spin with the effort of thinking of something to say, something different from what he'd come on purpose to say.

'How are you?' she asked.

'All right, thanks; I've been working. You managed to get away without any fuss, I hope?'

'Not exactly without any fuss.'

'Oh, I'm sorry to hear that. What happened?'

'I think Bertrand was rather suspicious. I told him there were one or two things I wanted to do in town. He said a lot of things about my being my own mistress, and I was to do what I wanted to do, and wasn't to feel I was tied in any way. It made me feel rather mean.'

'I can understand that.'

She leant forward and put her elbows on the low circular table between them. 'You see, Jim, in a way I think it was rather a bad thing my coming to meet you at all. But I'd said I would, and so I had to come. And, of course, I still wanted to, just as much as I did when you asked me. But I've been thinking it all over, and I've decided. . . . Look, shall we have our tea first, and then talk about it?'

'No, tell me now, whatever it is you want to say.'

'All right, then. It's this, Jim: I think I was a bit carried away by one thing and another then, when you asked me to come today, I mean. I think I wouldn't have said I'd come if I'd had time to think what I was doing. I'd still have wanted to come just as much. I'm sorry to have started this when we've hardly had time to say hullo to each other, but you can see what I'm going to say, can't you?'

Dixon didn't find himself thinking that this attitude would make it easier for him to do what he had to do. He said in a flat voice: 'You mean you don't want to go on with this?'

'It's just that I'm, oh, tied up with Bertrand, that's all. I don't want you to have the idea that I was being frivolous about you know—letting you kiss me, and saying I'd come today, and all that. And I meant everything I said; I wouldn't have said it otherwise. And I don't want you to think that I was doing it just for fun or that I've decided since that I don't like you enough, or anything like that. It's not like that, and you mustn't think it is.'

'That's all right, Christine. You can forget about that part of it. Oh . . . here it is.'

The waiter had come with a loaded tray. Christine began moving china about and pouring tea. When she gave him his cup she said: 'I'm sorry, Jim. I didn't want to be like this about it. Have a sandwich?'

'No, thanks. I don't want anything to eat.'

She nodded and began eating with all the signs of a good appetite. Dixon was interested by this absence of conventional feeling; for almost the first time in his life a woman was behaving in a way supposed to be typical of women. 'After all,' she said, 'you have your own ties with Margaret, haven't you?'

He sighed; although the worst part of the meeting was over in theory, without yet having had the effect he knew it soon would have on him, he still felt nervous. 'Yes,' he replied. 'That was what I was going to tell you about this afternoon, but you started first. I came here intending to tell you that I thought we shouldn't meet any more, so far as I'm concerned, because of my business with Margaret.'

'I see.' She began eating another sandwich.

'Things have all rather boiled over in the last few days, as a matter of fact. Since the Ball, really.'

She looked at him quickly. 'There was a row over that, was there?'

'Well, yes, I suppose you could say that. A good deal more than a row, actually.'

'How bad was it? What did she say to you?'

'Oh, she said all sorts of things. There wasn't much she could have said that she didn't say.'

'You make it sound rather terrible. What actually happened?'

Dixon sighed again and drank some tea. 'It's all so . . . complicated. I don't want to bore you with it.'

'You won't bore me. I'd like to hear, if you feel you want to tell me. It's your turn, after all.'

The grin she gave with this remark nearly left Dixon dumb. Was she really finding this funny? 'That's right,' he said heavily. 'Well, there's a lot of past history mixed up with it, you see. She's a good girl really, and I liked her a lot—at least, I would if she'd only let me. But I've got tied up with her without really meaning to, though I know that sounds ridiculous. When I first met her, last October, she was friendly with a fellow called Catchpole. . . .' He gave a shortened, but otherwise only slightly improved, account of his past relations with Margaret, finishing with their visit to the pictures the previous evening. Then he gave a cigarette to Christine, who'd eaten all the food the waiter had brought, took one himself, and said: 'So now it's all more or less as before, though I shouldn't like to have to explain what it is that's more or less as before.'

Christine was evidently not an experienced smoker. She coughed and said: 'Well, it seems as if we're both tied up, doesn't it? It's probably the best thing.'

Dixon's feeling of regret made him begin to talk fast. 'Yes, there's not much difference between us when you think about it. You're keeping your little affair with Bertrand going because you think that on the whole it's safer to do that than to take a risk with me. And I'm sticking to Margaret because I haven't got the courage to leave her to look after herself, so I do that instead of doing what I want to do, because I'm afraid to. It's just a sort of dull, lifeless caution that's the matter with us; you can't even call it looking after our own interests.'

She looked at him, her face reddening. 'I think it's silly to talk that way,' she said. 'You seem to think you've proved something by saying that. Of course that's what we're doing; you talk as if that's all we're doing. Don't you think people ever do things because they want to do them, because they want to do what's best? I don't see how it helps to call trying to do the right thing caution and lack of courage. You're the sort of man who'd never be happy whatever you did. I think I'll go now, Jim; there's not much sense in . . .'

'No, don't go,' Dixon said in distress. Things were happening much too fast for him. 'Don't be angry. Stay a little longer.'

'I'm not angry. I'm just fed up with it all.'

'Are we ever going to see each other again, then?'

'Once more, at least. I'm coming to your lecture, and to the sherry-party at the Principal's before it.'

'Oh, Heaven, Christine, you oughtn't to come to that. You'll be bored to tears. How did you get involved?'

'Uncle Julius has been asked by the Principal, and it seems he said he'd come in an unguarded moment, and now he insists on my coming to keep him company.'

'Rather queer.'

'He said he was looking forward to meeting you again.'

'Why on earth did he say that? I've hardly said two words to him.'

'Well, that's what he said. Don't ask me what he meant.'

'I shall see you at a distance, then, at least. That's good.'

Christine suddenly said in a different voice: 'No, it isn't good. How can it be? It'll be great fun, won't it? standing there chatting to Bertrand and Uncle Julius and the rest of them like a good little girl. Oh, yes, I shall be enjoying myself so much, thank you. . . . It's all so . . . It's unbearable.' She stood up and so did Dixon, who could find nothing to say. 'That's enough of that. This time I really am going. Thank you for the tea.'

'Give me your address, Christine.'

She looked at him scornfully, her brown eyes looking huge under the dark eyebrows. 'That'll do no good at all. What on earth would be the sense of it?'

'It would make me feel we hadn't seen each other for the last time.'

'Well, there's no sense in feeling that, is there?' She went quickly past him and out of the room without looking back.

CHAPTER 17

'What, finally, is the practical application of all this? Can anything be done to stop, or even hinder the process I have described? I say to you that something can be done by each one of us here tonight. Each of us can resolve to do something, every day, to speak against the false standards of today, to say one word for the simple, natural standards of the self-supporting village community. In that way we shall be saying a word, however small in its individual effect, for our native tradition, for our common heritage,

in short, for what we once had and may, some day, have
again—Merrie England.'

Making a long loud sound of disgust, Dixon got up from
the chair where he'd been writing this and did his ape
imitation all round the room and up on to the bed, where
he jumped up and down a few times, making noises to
himself. A knock at his door was followed so quickly by
the entrance of Bertrand that he only had time to stop
the noises and straighten his body.

Bertrand, who was wearing his blue beret, looked at
him. 'What are you doing up there?'

'I like being up here, thanks. Any objection?'

'Come down and stop playing the fool. I've got a few
things to say to you, and you'd better listen.' He seemed
to be in a controlled rage, and was breathing heavily,
though this might well have been the result of running up
the stairs.

Dixon jumped lightly down to the floor; he, too, was
panting a little. 'What do you want to say?'

'Just this. The last time I saw you, I told you to stay
away from Christine. I have discovered that you haven't
done so. What are you going to say about that?'

'What do you mean, I haven't stayed away from her?'

'Don't try that with me, Dixon. I know all about your
secret cup of tea with her yesterday.'

'Oh, she told you about that, did she?'

Bertrand tightened his lips behind the beard, which
looked as if it needed combing. 'No, no, of course she
didn't,' he said violently. 'If you knew her at all, you'd
know she didn't do things like that. She's not like you. If
you really want to know—and I hope it makes you happy
—it was your friend Johns who told my mother about it.
You ought to enjoy thinking about that. Everybody hates

you, Dixon, and by heaven I can see why. But the point is, I want an explanation of your behaviour. I gave you a clear warning to leave Christine alone. When I say that sort of thing, I expect people to have the sense to do as I say. Why haven't you? Eh?'

Bertrand's rage and his visit here combined nicely with the fact that both were unnecessary because Dixon had already given up his interest in Christine for other reasons. But he'd be a fool not to keep silent about that and enjoy himself with a bit of skirmishing. 'I didn't want to,' he said.

'Just get this into your so-called mind,' Bertrand raged. 'When I see something I want, I get it. I don't allow people of your sort to stand in my way. That's what you're forgetting. I'm having Christine because it's my right. Do you understand that?'

Dixon moved nearer. 'You're getting a bit too old to threaten like that, Welch,' he said quickly. 'People aren't going to stand aside for you for ever. You think that just because you're tall and can paint you're a sort of half-god. It wouldn't be so bad if you really were. But you're not: you're dishonest and a snob and a bully and a fool. And you're so dishonest that you can tell me that you're going to have Christine without remembering for a moment that you're in the middle of an affair with some other fellow's wife all the time.'

'What the hell are you talking about?' Bertrand's breath was whistling through his nose. He clenched his fists.

'Your bit of love-and-kisses with Carol Goldsmith. That's what I'm talking about.'

'If you ever tell this tale to Christine, I'll break your neck into so many . . .'

'*All right, you've asked for it,*' Bertrand bayed furiously.

'It's all right, I'm not the sort to do that,' Dixon said with a grin. 'I'm not like you. I can take Christine away from you without that.'

'All right, you've asked for it,' Bertrand bayed furiously. 'I warned you.'

Dixon took off his glasses and put them in his top jacket pocket.

They faced each other, feet apart and elbows bent in uncertain attitudes, as if about to begin some solemn ritual of which neither had learnt the movements. 'I'll teach you,' Bertrand panted and aimed a blow at Dixon's face. Dixon stepped aside, but his feet slipped and before he could recover, Bertrand's fist had landed with some force high up on his right cheek-bone. A little shaken, but still confident, Dixon stood still and, while Bertrand was still off balance after delivering his blow, hit him very hard indeed on the larger and uglier of his ears. Bertrand fell down, making a lot of noise in doing so and knocking down a china ornament. It exploded on the floor, to throw into contrast the silence which followed. Dixon stepped forward, rubbing his knuckles. The blow had hurt them rather. After some seconds, Bertrand began moving about on the floor, but made no attempt to get up. It was clear that Dixon had won. He put his glasses on again, feeling good.

A quiet knocking came at the door. 'Come in,' Dixon said.

Atkinson entered. 'Ha, Jim,' he said, then added politely, 'Good afternoon' to the still prostrate Bertrand, who, thus encouraged, struggled to his feet. 'I seem to have come at an inconvenient time.'

'Not at all,' Dixon said smoothly. 'Mr. Welch is just going.'

Bertrand shook his head, not in disagreement, but apparently to clear it, which interested Dixon. He moved host-like to the door with the departing Bertrand, who went out in silence.

CHAPTER 18

'I hope it isn't too painful, Dixon,' the Principal said.

Dixon's hand went up to his black eye. 'Oh no, sir,' he replied in a light tone. 'I'm surprised it's swollen at all, really. It was quite a light knock; didn't even break the skin.'

'On the corner of the wash-hand basin, you said?' another voice asked.

'That's right, Mr Gore-Urquhart. One of these silly things one does occasionally. I dropped my razor, bent down for it, and—bang!'

Gore-Urquhart nodded slowly. 'Most unfortunate,' he said. He looked Dixon up and down, and his lips seemed to be not quite under control. 'If I'd been asked, now,' he went on, 'I'd have said he'd been mixed up in a fight, eh, Principal?'

The fourth member of the group spoke. 'Well, I hope it won't interfere with your reading from your . . . from your . . .'

'Oh no, Professor,' Dixon said. 'I am sure I could read that script blindfold. I've been through it so many times.'

Welch nodded. 'It's a good plan,' he said. 'I remember when I first began lecturing, I was silly enough just to write the stuff down and not bother about . . .'

'Have you got anything new to tell us, Dixon?' the Principal asked.

Rescue came in the shape of the porter Maconochie with a tray of glasses of sherry. Dixon forced his hand to stay at his side until his three seniors had helped themselves, then let it bear the fullest remaining glass to his lips. He felt slightly ill in a way he couldn't name, but took half his new glassful in one swallow; it slid warmly down to join the previous three sherries and the half-dozen measures of Bill Atkinson's whisky. In a way, but only in a way, he was beginning not to worry about the lecture, which was to start in twenty minutes' time, at six-thirty.

He looked round the crowded Common Room, which seemed to contain everybody he knew or had ever known. One large group was made up of important local men, members of the College Council. The Principal moved over to this group, and almost at the same time a signal from Mrs Welch drew Welch away and left Dixon with Gore-Urquhart, who now said: 'How long have you been in this job, then, Dixon?'

'Almost nine months now. I got the job last autumn.'

'I've an idea you're not too happy in it; am I right?'

'Yes, I think you are right, on the whole.'

'Where's the trouble? In you or in it?'

'Oh, both, I think. They waste my time and I waste theirs.'

'Mm, I see. It's a waste of time teaching history, is it?'

Dixon resolved not to mind what he said to this man. 'No. Well taught and sensibly taught, history can do people a lot of good. But in practice that doesn't happen. Things get in the way. I don't quite see who's to blame for it. Bad teaching's the main thing. Not bad students, I mean.'

Gore-Urquhart nodded, then shot a quick glance at him. 'This lecture of yours tonight, now. Whose idea was it?'

'Professor Welch's. I couldn't refuse, of course. If it is a success it'll improve my position here.'

'You're ambitious?'

'No. I've done badly here since I got the job. This lecture might help to save me from getting the sack.'

'Here, lad,' Gore-Urquhart said, and snatched two glasses of sherry from Maconochie's tray as he went towards the group that now included the Principal. Dixon thought perhaps he oughtn't to drink any more—he was already beginning to feel a little splendid—but took the glass that was held out to him and drank from it. 'Why have you come here tonight?' he asked.

'I've made excuses to your Principal so many times recently that I felt I had to come to this.'

'I can't see why you bother, you know. You're not dependent on the Principal. You're only condemning yourself to a lot of boredom.'

When Gore-Urquhart looked at him again, Dixon had a moment's trouble getting rid of a slight spinning of the head, caused by the other's out-of-focus face. 'I condemn myself to several hours' boredom every day, Dixon. A couple more won't kill me.'

'Why do you do it?'

'I want to influence people so they'll do what I think it's important they should do. I can't get them to do that unless I let them bore me first, you understand. Then just as they're delighting in having made me half-stupid with talk I come back at them and make them do what I've decided they should do.'

'I wish I could do that,' Dixon said enviously. 'When I'm half-stupid with talk, which is what I am most of the

time, that's when they come at me and make me do what
they want me to do.' Nervousness and drink combined to
break through another barrier in his mind and he went on
eagerly: 'I'm the boredom-detector. I'm a delicately tuned
instrument. If only I could make myself known to a
millionaire I'd be worth a vast amount of money to him.
He could send me ahead into dinners and sherry-parties
and night-clubs, just for five minutes, and then by looking
at me he'd be able to read the boredom-degree of any
gathering. Like a cage-bird down a mine, same idea.'

Gore-Urquhart nodded. Two of the members of the
College Council now came over and drew him away to
join their group round the Principal. Dixon couldn't help
admiring the way in which, without saying or doing anything definite, they made it clear so effortlessly that he
himself wasn't expected to accompany them. He drained
his glass and went up to Christine and Bertrand. 'Hullo,
you two,' he cried gaily. 'Where have you been hiding?'

Christine flashed a look at Bertrand that made him not
say whatever he'd been going to say, and said herself:
'I'd no idea this was going to be such a grand affair. Half
the top men in the city must be here.'

'I'd like us to go to your uncle now, Christine,' Bertrand
said. 'There are one or two things I want to discuss with
him, if you remember.'

'In a minute, Bertrand; there's plenty of time,' Christine
said.

'No no, there isn't plenty of time; the thing's due to
start in about ten minutes, and that isn't plenty of time
for what I want to talk about.'

'Why, hullo, Bertie dear,' Carol said behind him. 'I
want you. Come over here, will you?'

Bertrand had performed a jump of surprise and half-turn in one movement. 'Hullo, Carol, but I was just . . .'

'I shan't keep you a minute,' Carol said, and gripped his arm. 'I'll give him back in good condition,' she added over her shoulder to Christine.

'Well . . . hullo, Christine,' Dixon said.

'Oh, hullo.'

'This really is the last time, isn't it?'

'Yes, that's right.'

He felt childish anger and self-pity. 'You don't seem to mind as much as I do.'

She looked at him for a moment, then quickly turned her head away, as if he were showing her a photograph in a medical book. 'I've done all my minding,' she said. 'I'm not going to do any more now. Neither will you if you've got any sense.'

'I can't help minding,' he said. 'Minding isn't a thing you can do anything about. I can't help going on minding.'

'What's the matter with your eye?'

'Bertrand and I had a fight this afternoon.'

'A fight? He didn't say anything to me about it. What were you fighting about? A fight?'

'He told me to stay away from you, and I said I wouldn't, so we started fighting.'

'But we agreed. . . . You haven't changed your mind about . . . ?'

'No. I just wasn't going to let him tell me what to do, that's all.'

'But imagine having a fight.' She seemed to be keeping back a laugh. 'You lost, by the look of you.'

He didn't like that, and remembered her almost grinning during the hotel tea. 'Not at all. Take a look at Bertrand's ear before you start deciding who won and who lost.'

'Which one?'

'The right. But there probably won't be much to see. The damage was mostly internal, I should think.'

'Did you knock him over?'

'Oh, yes. Right over. He stayed down for a bit, too.'

'Heaven.' She stared at him, her full, dry lips slightly apart. A pang of helpless desire made Dixon feel heavy and immovable, as if he were being talked to by Welch.

In the moment of silence, Bertrand suddenly reappeared. His face was red. 'That's enough of that,' he said, his voice a choking bay. 'This is just how I expected things to be.' He caught hold of Christine's arm and pulled her away with some violence. Before moving away, he said to Dixon: 'All right, my lad. This is the finish for you. You'd better start looking for another job. I mean that.' Christine gave Dixon a brief, frightened glance over her shoulder as she was marched away towards the group that contained her uncle.

What he'd warned himself of at the beginning had really happened; he'd let the joy of battle rob him of his wisdom and caution. He was helpless; above all, helpless to prevent that bearded fool from standing there with his hand on Christine's arm, confident, victorious. She stood by her boy-friend, in an awkward uncomfortable attitude, even an ungraceful one, but so far as Dixon was concerned there could be no more beautiful way for a woman to stand.

'Taking your last look, eh, James?'

At this sudden appearance of Margaret from behind him, Dixon felt like a man fighting a policeman who sees another approaching on a horse. 'What?' he said.

'You'd better have a good look at her, hadn't you? You won't get another chance.'

'No, I don't suppose I . . .'

'Unless, of course, you've arranged to go up to London from time to time, just to keep in touch.'

Dixon stared into her face, genuinely surprised, surprised too that Margaret could, at this stage, do anything to surprise him. 'What do you mean?' he asked dully.

'There's no use pretending, is there? It doesn't take much imagination to see what you're thinking.' The end of her nose moved slightly as she talked, in the way it always did. She stood with her feet apart, as Dixon had seen her many times, making small-talk in this room or one of the little teaching-rooms upstairs. She didn't look at all strained, or excited, or uncomfortable or annoyed.

Dixon gave a sigh of weariness before setting out on the kind of protests and excuses laid down for him by the conventions of this particular game.

With no conclusion reached, their conversation was brought to an end by the drift of the Principal's group towards the door. Gore-Urquhart was apparently deep in talk with Bertrand and Christine. Welch called: 'Ready, Dixon?'

'See you in the Hall, Professor,' Dixon called back; then, with a word to Margaret, he hurried out and into the Staff Cloakroom. Stage-fright was upon him now; his hands were cold and damp, his legs felt like soft rubber tubes filled with fine sand, he had difficulty in controlling his breathing. He was trying to deal with this by making one of his worst madman faces when he found himself face to face with Gore-Urquhart. He straightened his eyes and mouth, and said 'Oh, hullo.'

'Hullo, Dixon,' Gore-Urquhart said, then stood gazing at him. After a moment, he said: 'Are you perhaps feeling a little nervous, lad?'

'Very nervous.'

Gore-Urquhart nodded and produced a good-sized flask. 'Take a swallow.'

'Thanks.' Deciding not to bother about coughing, Dixon took a good draw at what was evidently full-strength Scotch whisky—more evidently than any drink he'd ever had. He coughed wildly.

'Yes, it's good stuff, that. Have another swallow.'

'Thanks.' Dixon did exactly as before, then, struggling for breath and wiping his mouth on the back of his hand, gave the flask back. 'I'm very grateful for that.'

'It'll do you a lot of good. Well, we had better go if we don't want to keep them waiting.'

The last of the guests were still leaving the Common Room and moving up the stairs. At the top of the stairs a little group was waiting: the Goldsmiths, Bertrand, Christine, Welch, and the other lecturers in the History Department.

They began moving into the Hall, which was frighteningly full. The front row of the gallery held an unbroken line of students. There was a loud mixture of conversations.

'Well, best of luck, Jim,' Carol said. Others echoed her words, and they all moved away into their seats.

'Here you go, then, lad,' Gore-Urquhart said in a low voice. 'No need to worry; to hell with all this.' He gripped Dixon's arm and then moved away.

Dixon followed Welch on to the platform. The Principal and the fattest members of the College Council were already there. Dixon found that he felt rather drunk.

CHAPTER 19

Welch uttered the introductory braying sound, a relative of his son's bay, with which he was accustomed to call for silence at the start of a lecture. Dixon had heard students imitating it. A silence gradually resulted. 'We are here tonight,' he informed the audience, 'to listen to a lecture.'

While Welch talked, his body swaying to and fro, its upper half more strongly lit by the reading-lamp above the lecture-stand, Dixon, so as not to have to listen to what was said, looked secretly round the Hall. It was certainly very full; a few rows at the back had fewer inhabitants, but those nearer the front were packed, chiefly with members of Staff and their families and with local people of various degrees of importance. The gallery, as far as Dixon could see, was also packed; some people were standing up by the wall at the back. Dropping his eyes to the nearer seats, Dixon saw most of those who had been in the Common Room a few minutes ago. Before he could look further, his feeling of illness was upon him again; a wave of heat spread from his back to the top of his head. To prevent himself from groaning, he tried to force himself to feel all right; only the nervousness, he told himself. And the drink, of course.

When Welch said '. . . Mr Dixon,' and sat down, Dixon stood up. His knees began shaking violently. A loud thunder of applause started up, chiefly, it seemed, from the gallery. With some difficulty, he took his position at the lecture-stand, looked quickly at his first sentence and raised his head. The applause died away slightly, enough for sounds of laughter to be heard through it; then it gathered force again, soon becoming louder than before. The part of the audience in the gallery had had its first clear view of Dixon's black eye.

Several heads were being turned in the first few rows, and the Principal, Dixon saw, was staring rather angrily at the area of disturbance. In his own general discomfort, Dixon, who could never understand afterwards how or why he did it, produced an excellent imitation of Welch's introductory braying sound. The uproar, passing the point where it could still be considered as applause, grew louder. The Principal rose slowly to his feet. The uproar died down, though not to complete silence. After a pause, the Principal nodded to Dixon and sat down.

Dixon's blood rushed in his ears. How could he stand up here in front of them all and try to talk? What further animal noises would come out of his mouth if he did? He smoothed the edge of his script and began.

When he'd spoken about half a dozen sentences, Dixon realised that something was still very wrong. The murmuring in the gallery had grown a little louder. Then he realised what it was that was so wrong: he'd gone on using Welch's style of lecturing. And now, as this flashed into his struggling mind, he began to trip on one or two phrases, to hesitate, and to repeat words, even to lose his place once so that a ten-second pause occurred. The increasing murmur from the gallery showed that these effects were not passing unappreciated. Red and sweating, he struggled on a little further, hearing Welch's tones wrapping themselves tightly round his voice, powerless for the moment to get rid of them. A wave of drunkenness across his brain informed him of the arrival there of the advance-guard of Gore-Urquhart's whisky—or was it only that last sherry? And how hot it was. He stopped speaking, prepared his mouth for a tone as different from Welch's as possible, and started again. Everything seemed all right for the moment.

As he talked, he began glancing round the front rows. He saw Gore-Urquhart sitting next to Bertrand, who had his mother on the other side. Christine sat on the far side of her uncle, with Carol next to her, then Cecil. Margaret was at the other end, next to Mrs Welch, but with her glasses reflecting the light so that he couldn't see whether she was looking at him or not. He noticed that Christine was whispering something to Carol, and seemed to be worried about something. So that this shouldn't make him break down again, he looked further back, trying to pick out Bill Atkinson. Yes, there he was, by the central aisle about half-way back. Over the whisky-bottle an hour and a half earlier, Atkinson had insisted, not only on coming to the lecture, but on announcing his intention of pretending to faint if Dixon, finding things getting too difficult in any way, should scratch both his ears at the same time. 'It'll be a good faint,' Atkinson had said. Recalling this now, Dixon had to fight down a burst of laughter. At the same moment, a disturbance nearer the platform attracted his attention: Christine and Carol were pushing past the others with the clear intention of leaving the Hall. Dixon found himself unable to go on talking.

When he recovered himself, he found that he'd once more lost his place in mid-sentence. Biting his lip, he resolved not to get lost again. He cleared his throat, found his place, and went on, making each word separate and very clear, and keeping his voice well up at the end of each sentence. At least, he thought, they'll hear every word now. As he went on, he was for the second time conscious of something being very wrong. It was some moments before he realised that he was now imitating the Principal.

He looked up; there seemed to be a lot of movement in the gallery. Something heavy crashed to the floor up there. Maconochie, who'd been standing near the doors, went out—to go up there and restore order, Dixon supposed. Voices were now starting to come from the body of the Hall. 'What's the matter with you, Dixon?' Welch asked in a loud whisper.

'Sorry,   sir . . . bit   nervous . . . all   right   in   a minute. . . .'

He began to read again, and things began slowly to go wrong for the third time, but not, as before, with what he was saying or how he was saying it. These things had to do with the inside of his head. A feeling, not so much of drunkenness, but of immense sorrow and tiredness, was settling there. While he spoke one sentence, sadness at the thought of Christine seemed to be trying to grip his tongue and make it impossible to speak; while he spoke another, cries of angry horror groped in his throat, seeking to make public what he felt about the Margaret situation; while he spoke the next, anger and fear threatened to twist his mouth, tongue, and lips into the right position for a hysterical denunciation of Bertrand, Mrs Welch, the Principal, the College Council, the College. He began to lose all consciousness of the audience; the only member of it he cared about had left and was not, he supposed, going to come back. Well, if this was going to be his last public appearance here, he'd make sure that people didn't forget it quickly. He'd do some good, however small, to some of those present, however few. No more imitations, they frightened him too much, but he could suggest by his tones, very subtly of course, what his opinion was of his subject and the worth of the statements he was making.

Gradually, but not as gradually as it seemed to some parts of his brain, he began to slip into his tones a sarcastic, wounding bitterness. Nobody who wasn't mad, he tried to suggest, could take seriously a single word of this boring mixture of guessing and rubbish. A growing mutter, half-amused, half-indignant, rose about him, but he closed his ears to it and read on. Almost unconsciously he began to adopt an unnameable foreign pronunciation and to read faster and faster, his head spinning. As if in a dream he heard Welch moving, then whispering, then talking at his side. He began to introduce muffled snorts of mockery into his speech. He read on, spitting out the words like curses, leaving mispronunciations and omissions uncorrected, turning over the pages of his script like a musician reading a fast movement, raising his voice higher and higher. At last he found his final paragraph in front of his eyes, stopped, and looked at his audience.

Below him, the members of the College Council were staring at him with frozen astonishment and protest. The senior members of the Staff looked up with similar expressions; the junior members wouldn't look up at all. The only person in the main body of the hall who was actually producing sounds was Gore-Urquhart, and the sounds he was producing were of loud joyful laughter. Shouts, whistles and applause came from the gallery. Dixon raised his hand for silence, but the noise continued. It was too much; he felt faint again, and put his hands over his ears. Through all the noise a louder noise made itself heard, something between a groan and a roar. Half-way down the Hall, Bill Atkinson, unable at that distance, or unwilling, to distinguish between the scratching and the covering of ears, collapsing like a falling tree in the aisle. The Principal

'That's enough, Dixon,' the Principal said loudly.

rose to his feet, opening and shutting his mouth, but without any quietening effect. The people near Atkinson started trying to lift him up, but in vain. Welch began calling Dixon's name. A stream of students entered and moved towards the prostrate Atkinson. There were perhaps twenty or thirty of them. Shouting directions and advice to one another, they picked him up and bore him through the doors. Dixon came round in front of the lecture-stand and the uproar died away. 'That's enough, Dixon,' the Principal said loudly, signalling to Welch, but too late.

'What, finally, is the practical application of all this?' Dixon said in his normal voice. He heard himself talking without consciously calling any words up. 'Listen and I'll tell you. The point about Merrie England is that it was about the most un-Merrie period in our history. It's only the simple-life, arty people of today . . .' He paused and swayed; the heat, the drink, the nervousness, the guilt at last joined forces in him. His head seemed to be swelling and growing lighter at the same time; his body felt as if it were being ground out into its original particles; his ears hummed and his eyes were playing tricks. Chairs scraped at each side of him; a hand caught at him, and with Welch's arm round his shoulders he sank to his knees, half-hearing the Principal's voice saying above the uproar: '. . . from finishing his lecture through sudden indisposition. I'm sure you'll all . . .'

I've done it now, he managed to think. And without even telling them. . . . He drew air into his lungs; if he could push it out again he'd be all right, but he couldn't, and everything faded out in a great roar of wordless voices.

E

CHAPTER 20

When Dixon went in through the College gates next morning, three students standing there fell silent and nudged each other.

His stomach turned over as he recognised Welch's handwriting on a note with his mail. He went upstairs reading it. Welch felt he ought to let him know, unofficially, that when the Council met next week he would be unable to recommend keeping Dixon on the Staff. He advised Dixon, also unofficially, to settle his affairs in the district and leave as soon as possible. He would supply testimonials for any application Dixon might make for a new job, so long as it was outside the city. He himself was sorry Dixon had got to leave, because he'd enjoyed working with him.

Dixon went into his room and stood at the window. He could easily get a schoolteaching job; his old headmaster had told him at Christmas that a senior history post in the school wouldn't be filled until September. He'd write to him and say he'd decided University teaching didn't suit him. But he wouldn't write today, not today.

Moving off down College Road with his books and notes under his left arm, Dixon forgot to take a last look at the College buildings until it was too late. He felt almost free from care, which, considering the circumstances, was something he thought he could be proud of. He'd go home that afternoon and come back next week to get the last of his possessions, see Margaret, and so on. See Margaret. 'Ooooeeeeyaaa,' he called out to himself, thinking of it. 'Waaaeeeeoooghgh.' With his home so near hers, leaving this place wouldn't seem like a move on, but a drift to one side. That was really the worst of it.

He remembered now that this was the day he was to see Catchpole at lunch-time. What could the fellow want? No use wondering about that; the important thing was how to fill in the time until then. Back at his lodgings, he bathed his eye, which was beginning to fade a little, though its new colour was just as unpleasant. Then he had a shave and a bath. While he was in the water, he heard the telephone ring, and in a few moments Miss Cutler knocked at the door. 'Are you there, Mr Dixon?'

'Yes, what is it, Miss Cutler?'

'A gentleman on the telephone for you.'

'Who is it?'

'I'm afraid I didn't hear the name.'

'Oh, all right, Miss Cutler. Would you ask him for his number and say I'll ring him up in about ten minutes?'

Dixon dried himself, wondering who this could be. When he reached the telephone, he found a note with the number, but the name had again been too difficult. A woman's voice answered the telephone, announcing the number.

'Have you got a man there?' Dixon asked, not knowing what else to say.

'A man? Who's that speaking?' The tone was hostile.

'My name's Dixon.'

'Oh yes, Mr Dixon, of course. One moment, please.'

There was a brief pause, then a man's voice said: 'Hullo. That you, Dixon?'

'Yes, speaking. Who's that?'

'Gore-Urquhart. Got the sack, have you?'

'What?'

'I said, got the sack?'

'Yes.'

'Good. I was told it in confidence so I am glad I haven't

got to tell you. Well, what are your plans, Dixon?'

'I was thinking of trying schoolteaching.'

'Are you keen to?'

'No, not really.'

'Good. I've got a job for you. Five hundred pounds a year. You'll have to start at once, on Monday. It'll mean living in London. You accept?'

Dixon found that he could not only breathe, but talk. 'What job is it?'

'Sort of private secretary. Not much letter-writing; a young woman does most of that. It'll be mainly meeting people or telling people I can't meet them. We'll go into details on Monday morning. Ten o'clock at my house in London. Write down the address.' He gave it, then asked: 'Are you all right, now?'

'Oh, yes, thanks. I went to bed as soon as I . . .'

'No, I wasn't enquiring about your health, man. Have you got all the details? You'll be there on Monday?'

'Yes, of course, and thank you very much, Mr. . . .'

'Right, then, I'll see you. . . .'

'Just a moment, Mr Gore-Urquhart. Shall I be working with Bertrand Welch?'

'Whatever gave you that idea?'

'Nothing; I just heard he was trying to get a job with you.'

'That's the job you've got. I knew young Welch was no good as soon as I saw him. Just like his pictures. It's a great pity he's managed to get my niece tied up with him, a great pity. No use saying anything to her, though. Still. I think you'll do the job all right, Dixon. It's not that you've got the qualifications. But you haven't got the dis-qualifications, and that's much rarer. Any more questions?'

'No, that's all, thank you, I . . .'

'Ten o'clock Monday.' He rang off.

Dixon rose slowly from the telephone table. What noise could he make to express the mixture in him of awe and the desire to laugh like a madman. He drew in his breath for a growl of happiness, but was recalled to everyday affairs by a single hasty note from the clock. It was twelve-thirty, the time he was supposed to be meeting Catchpole to discuss Margaret.

CHAPTER 21

Catchpole, already there when Dixon arrived, turned out to be a tall, thin young man in his early twenties who looked like a don trying to look like a bank-clerk. He got Dixon a drink, apologised to him for taking up his time, and, after a few more polite remarks, said: 'I think the best thing I can do is give you the true facts of this matter. Do you agree with that?'

'Yes, all right, but how shall I know that they are the true facts?'

'You won't, of course. Except that if you know Margaret you can't fail to recognise that they are likely. Firstly, contrary to what Margaret seems to have told you, she and I were never lovers in any meaning of the word. That's news to you, I suppose?'

'Yes,' Dixon said. He felt curiously frightened, as if Catchpole were trying to start a quarrel with him.

'I thought it might be. Well, having met her at a political meeting, I found myself, without quite knowing how, going about with her, taking her to the theatre and to the pictures, and all that kind of thing. Quite soon I realised that she was one of these people—they're usually women—who feed on emotional tension. We began to have rows about nothing—really about nothing. I was much too cautious, of course, to make love to her in any way, but she soon started behaving as if I had. I was always being accused of hurting her, taking no notice of her, and all that kind of thing. Have you had any experiences of that sort with her?'

'Yes,' Dixon said. 'Go on.'

'I can see that you and I have more in common than we thought at first. Well, after a particularly stupid row about some remark I'd made when introducing her to my sister, I decided I didn't want any more of that kind of thing. I told her so. It was terrible.' Catchpole combed his hair back with his fingers and moved uncomfortably in his chair. 'I'd got the afternoon free and we were out shopping, I remember, and she started shouting at me in the street. It was really dreadful. I felt I couldn't bear another minute of it, so finally, to keep her quiet, I agreed to go round and see her that evening about ten o'clock. When the time came, I couldn't bear the idea of going. A couple of days later, when I found out about her . . . attempted suicide, I realised that that was the evening I'd been expected to go and see her. It gave me a bit of a shock when I realised I could have prevented it all if I'd taken the trouble to go.'

'Wait a minute,' Dixon said with a dry mouth. 'She asked me to go there that evening as well. She told me afterwards that you'd come and told her . . .'

Catchpole interrupted. 'Are you quite sure? Are you sure it was that evening?'

'Absolutely. I can remember the whole thing quite
clearly. As a matter of fact, we'd just been buying the
sleeping pills when she asked me to come, the pills she
must have used in the evening. That's how I remember.
Why, what's the matter?'

'She bought some sleeping pills when she was with you?'

'Yes, that's right.'

'When was this?'

'That she bought them? Oh, about midday I suppose.
Why?'

Catchpole said slowly: 'But she bought a bottle of pills
while she was with me in the afternoon.'

They looked at each other in silence. 'I imagine she
copied the doctor's signature,' Dixon said finally.

'We were both expected to be there, then, and see what
we'd driven her to,' Catchpole said bitterly. 'I knew she
was neurotic, but not as neurotic as that.'

'It was lucky for her the man in the room underneath
came up to complain about her radio.'

'She wouldn't have taken a risk like that. No, this
almost proves what I've always thought. Margaret had no
intention of committing suicide, then or at any other
time. She must have taken some of the pills before we
were due to arrive—not enough to kill her of course—and
waited for us to rush in and tear our hair and attend to
her and blame ourselves. I don't think there can be any
doubt of that. She was never in any danger of dying at all.'

'But there's no proof of that,' Dixon said.

'Can't you see? It's the only explanation that fits. Try
to remember; did she say anything about how many pills
she took?'

'No, I don't think so. I just remember her saying she
was holding on to the empty bottle all the time she . . .'

'The empty bottle. There were two bottles. That's it. I'm satisfied now. I was right.'

'Have another drink,' Dixon said. He felt he must get away from Catchpole for a moment, but while he was standing at the bar he found he couldn't think, all he could do was to try vainly to get his thoughts into order.

As soon as he returned with the drinks, Catchpole said: 'You're not still doubtful, I hope? The empty bottle. But there were two bottles, and she only used one. How do I know? Do you imagine she'd have failed to tell you she'd used two if she had used two? No, she forgot to tell a lie there. She thought it wouldn't matter. She couldn't guess that I might talk to you. I can't blame her for that: even the best planner can't think of everything. She'd have made sure, of course, that she'd be in no danger with one bottle. Perhaps two bottles wouldn't have killed her, either, but she wasn't taking any risks.' He picked up his drink and swallowed half of it. 'Well, I'm extremely grateful to you for doing this for me. I'm completely free of her now. No more worrying about how she is, thank heaven.' He gazed at Dixon with his hair falling over his brow. 'And you're free of her too, I hope.'

'You didn't ever mention the question of marriage to her, did you?'

'No, I wasn't foolish enough for that. She told you I did, I suppose?'

'Yes. And you didn't go off to Wales with a girl about that time either?'

'Unfortunately not. I went to Wales, yes, but that was for my company. They don't provide their representatives with girls to go away with, unluckily.' He finished his drink and stood up, quieter now. 'I hope I've removed your suspicions of me. I've been very glad to meet you, and I'd like to thank you for what you've done.' He leaned forward and lowered his voice further. 'Don't try to help her any more; it's too dangerous for you. I know what I'm talking about. She doesn't need any help either, you know, really. The best of luck to you. Good-bye.'

Dixon finished his drink and left a couple of minutes later. He went back towards his lodgings through the lunch-time crowds. All the facts seemed to fit, but Margaret had fixed herself too firmly in his life and his emotions to be pushed out of them by a mere list of facts. It would need something stronger than facts or he knew he would come to disbelieve this lot altogether.

Entering the dining-room, he found Bill Atkinson sitting at the table, reading. He looked up at Dixon. 'Just had your popsy on the telephone,' he said. 'Not that one. Christine. The main message is her train goes at one-fifty. I didn't get it all. She said she had some news for you that she couldn't tell me on the telephone, and that if you wanted to see her again you could see her off on this one-fifty train. She said she'd "understand" if you didn't come. Don't ask me what that means.' He looked at his notes and added that the train was leaving, not from the main city station, but from the smaller one near the Welchs' house. Some trains from other places stopped at this station on their way towards London.

'I'd better get moving, then,' Dixon said, making calculations.

'Yes. I'll tell Miss Cutler you won't want lunch. Go and get on that bus.' Atkinson lowered his face towards his paper.

Dixon ran out into the street. He felt as if he'd been hurrying all his life. Why wasn't she getting a train from the city station? There was an excellent one to London at

three-twenty, he knew. What was her news? In any case, he
had some for her; two lots in fact. Did her going so suddenly mean that she and Bertrand had had another row?
A bus was due to turn up College Road between one-ten and
one-fifteen. It was that time now. The next was at one-
thirty-five. Hopeless. He ran faster. No, she wouldn't have
left just because of a row. She wasn't like that. Oh, hell,
her news was probably just that 'Uncle Julius' was going
to offer him a job. Would she have asked him to come so
far just to tell him that? Or was it just an excuse for
seeing him again? But why should she want to do that?

When he saw the bus, it had stopped about fifty yards
away up College Road, and someone had just got on.
Dixon broke into a wild, lung-bursting run, while the
conductor watched him from the platform at the back.
When he was half-way to the bus, this official rang the
bell, the driver let in the clutch, and the wheels began to
turn. Dixon found he was even better at running than
he'd thought, but when the gap between man and bus
had narrowed to perhaps five yards, it began to widen
rapidly. Dixon stopped running and made the oldest rude
gesture in the world to the conductor, who was still calmly
watching. At once the conductor rang the bell again and
the bus stopped. Dixon hesitated for a moment, then ran
and got on with some embarrassment. He found himself
unwilling to meet the eye of the conductor, who now said
admiringly 'Well run, brother' and rang the bell for the
third time.

Dixon panted a question about the bus's time of arrival
at the station, which was where it ended its run, got a
civil answer which avoided giving exact information, and
climbed with an effort to the top deck. There he made his
rebounding way to the front seat and collapsed into it

without being able to afford the breath to groan. He looked out of the window; the road unfolded itself in front of him, and he couldn't help feeling some sort of happy excitement, especially at the brightness of the sunlit scene. Beyond the lines of houses open fields were already appearing, and through some trees he could see a gleam of water.

Christine had said that she'd 'understand' if he failed to come and see her off. What did that mean? Did it mean that she 'understood' that his ties with Margaret would have made him decide not to come? He couldn't allow Christine to escape him today; if she did he might not see her again at all. Not at all; that was an unhappy phrase. Suddenly his face changed, seeming to become all nose and glasses; the bus had moved up behind a lorry slowly drawing along a complicated trailer, which had a notice on it recommending caution and saying how many feet long it was. A smaller notice gave a further brief reason for caution: *Air brakes*. Lorry, trailer, and bus began moving, at a steady twelve miles an hour, round a long series of bends. With difficulty Dixon snatched his gaze from the back of the trailer and, to keep up his spirits, began thinking about what Catchpole had said to him about Margaret.

He realised at once that his mind had been made up as soon as he decided to make this journey. For the first time he really felt that it was no use trying to save those who by their nature did not want to be saved. It was all very unfortunate for Margaret, and was probably the result, as he'd thought before, of her being physically unattractive. Christine's more normal character was no doubt the result, in part at least, of her having been lucky with her face and figure. But that was as far as you could go. To say that differences were the result of luck wasn't the same thing as saying that they didn't exist. Still Christine was nicer and prettier than Margaret, and that fact led to many other things: there was no end to the ways in which nice things are nicer than nasty ones. It had been luck, too, that had freed him from pity's sticky trap; if Catchpole had been a different sort of man, he, Dixon, would still be caught as firmly as before.

The conductor now appeared and went through the business of selling Dixon a ticket. When this was over, he said: 'One forty-three we're due at the station. I looked it up in the book.'

'Oh. Shall we be punctual, do you think?'

'Couldn't say, I'm sorry. Not if we keep crawling behind this Air Force thing we shan't, I shouldn't think. Train to catch?'

'Well, I want to see someone who's travelling on the one-fifty.'

'Shouldn't be too sure of it if I were you.' He stayed there, no doubt to examine Dixon's black eye.

'Thanks,' Dixon said in a tone of dismissal.

They entered a long stretch of straight road, with a slight dip in the middle so that every yard of its empty surface could be seen. Far ahead the lorry driver's thin brown hand appeared and made a beckoning movement. The driver of the bus ignored this invitation and pulled to the left at a bus-stop.

When the gap between the bus and the lorry began to grow less again, Dixon found that his one interest in life was centred in the matter of the bus's progress; he no longer wondered what Christine would say to him if he got there in time, nor what he'd do if he didn't. He just sat there stretching his face in a fresh direction at each overtaking car, each bend, each unnecessary piece of caution in the driving.

The bus was now once more securely behind the trailer, which began to reduce speed even further. Before Dixon could cry out, before he'd time to guess what was going to happen, the lorry and trailer had moved off to the side into a lay-by and the bus was travelling on alone. Now was the time, he thought with returning hope, for the driver to start hurrying because of the time that had been lost. The driver evidently did not agree. Dixon lit a cigarette, attacking the side of the box with the match as if it were the driver's eye. Just then the bus turned a corner, slowed down, then stopped. Making a lot of noise, a farm tractor was pulling straight across the road something that looked like the springs of a giant's bed, caked in places with earth and bearing ribbons of grass. Dixon thought he really would have to run downstairs and attack both drivers with a knife; what next? what next? With loud grinding noises, the bus crept on, while every few yards groups of old men waited to climb slowly and painfully in.

As the traffic thickened slightly towards the town, the driver added to his extremes of caution an unbelievable care for the interests of other road-users; the sight of anything between an ancient van and junior bicycle halved his speed to four miles an hour. Before the bus had reached the station stop Dixon plunged down, out, across the road, and into the station entrance. The clock over the ticket-office pointed to one forty-seven. At once the minute hand jumped one space on. Dixon threw himself at the barrier. A hard-faced man stood in front of him.

'Which platform for London, please?'

The man looked at him. 'Bit early, aren't you?'

'What?'

'Next train to London's eight-seventeen.'

'Eight-seventeen?'

'No restaurant car.'

'What about the one-fifty?'

'No one-fifty. You haven't got it mixed up with the one-forty, have you?'

Dixon swallowed. 'I think I must have done,' he said. 'Thanks.'

'Sorry.'

Nodding mechanically, Dixon turned away. Bill Atkinson must have made a mistake in Christine's message. But it wasn't like Atkinson to make mistakes of that sort. Perhaps it had been Christine who'd made the mistake. It didn't really matter. He walked slowly to the entrance and stood looking out from the shadows at the little sunlit square. He still had his job. And it wouldn't be very difficult to get in touch with Christine. It was only that he felt it would be too late when he did. But at least he'd met her and talked to her a few times. He was thankful for that.

As he watched, wondering what to do next, he caught sight of a car with a damaged wing moving uncertainly round a Post Office van. Something about this car held Dixon's attention. It began to move towards him, roaring like a tractor. The roar was cut off by a terrible grinding of metal parts and the car came to a sudden stop. A tallish blonde girl wearing a wine-coloured jacket and skirt and carrying a raincoat and a large suitcase got out and began hurrying towards the place where Dixon stood.

Dixon moved out of sight behind a pillar, as quickly as he could under the attack of what must surely be a tearing of the stomach muscles. How could he, of all people, have ignored the importance of Welch's car-driving habits?

CHAPTER 22

Another uproar of mechanical rage outside told him that Welch was still at the wheel. Good; perhaps he had received orders to return without delay. Dixon had no feelings or thoughts beyond the present situation. He heard Christine's steps approaching and tried to press himself back into the pillar. Her feet took a few steps on the boards of the entrance-hall; she came into view four or five feet away, turned her head, and saw him at once. Her face broke into a smile of what seemed to him pure affection. 'You got my message, then,' she said. She looked ridiculously pretty.

'Come here, Christine, quickly.' He drew her into the shelter of his pillar. 'Just a moment.'

She stared about her and then at him. 'But we ought to be running up on to the platform. My train's nearly due.'

'Your train's gone. You'll have to wait for the next.'

'That clock says I've got one more minute. I can just . . .'

'No, it's gone, I tell you. It went at one-forty.'

'It couldn't have done.'

'It could and did. I asked the man.'

'But Mr Welch said it went at one-fifty.'

'Oh he did, did he? That explains everything. He was wrong about that, you see.'

'Are you sure? Why are we hiding? Are we hiding?'

Ignoring her, his hand unnoticed on her arm, Dixon leant carefully past her. Welch had now somehow got his car right across the road, blocking the entrance to the station. 'Good. Well we'll just give the silly old fool time to get clear, and then we'll go and have a drink.' He would

'You got my message then,' she said.

begin with a double double double whisky. 'You've had lunch, I suppose.'

'Yes, but I could hardly eat anything.'

'Not like you, that. Well, I haven't had any, so we'll have some together. I know a hotel not far from here. I used to go there with Margaret in the old days.'

They left Christine's suitcase in the luggage-office and walked out into the square. 'A good thing old Welch didn't insist on putting you on the train,' Dixon said.

'Yes. . . . Actually I was the one who insisted.'

'I don't blame you.' Dixon's physical discomfort grew steadily at the thought of Christine's 'news', soon to be revealed, it seemed. He wanted to assure himself that it would be bad so that there might be a chance of its being good.

'I wanted to get away as quickly as I could from the whole lot of them. I couldn't bear any of them for another moment. A fresh one arrived last night.'

'A fresh one?'

'Yes, Mitchell or some such name.'

'Oh, I know. You mean Michel.'

'Do I? I picked the first train I could get.'

'What's happened? That you wanted to tell me.' He tried to force his spirits down, to expect nothing but unexpected and very nasty nastiness.

She looked at him, and he again noticed that the white's of her eyes were a very light blue. 'I've finished with Bertrand.' She spoke as if a household washing-powder had been found unsatisfactory.

'Why? Permanently?'

'Yes. Do you want to hear about it?'

'Come on.'

'You remember me and Carol Goldsmith leaving your lecture in the middle yesterday?'

Dixon understood, and felt breathless. 'I know. She told you something, didn't she? I know what she told you.'

Without realising it they stopped walking. Dixon put out his tongue at an old woman who was staring at them. Christine said: 'You knew about Bertrand and her all the time, didn't you? I knew you did.' She looked as if she were going to laugh.

'Yes. What made her tell you?'

'Why didn't you tell me?'

'I couldn't. It wouldn't have done me any good. What made Carol tell you?'

'She hated him for taking her for granted. I didn't mind what he'd done before he started going about with me, but it was wrong of him to try to keep us both dancing round him. She said he asked her to come away with him the night we all went to the theatre. He was quite sure she would. She said she began by hating me and then she saw the way he was treating me, things like the way he behaved at that sherry thing. Then she saw he was the one to blame, not me.'

She stood with her shoulders a little forward, saying all this quickly and with embarrassment, her back to a shop-window full of garments for controlling the figure. He could see she was wondering whether she'd said enough to satisfy his curiosity.

He took Christine's arm and walked off with her. 'That's enough,' he said.

'There's a lot more about what he told her about . . .'

'Later.' A grin of happiness split Dixon's face. He said: 'I think you might like to hear this. I am going to have

nothing more to do with Margaret. Something's happened
—never mind what just now—which means I needn't
bother with her any more.'

'What, you mean you're absolutely . . . ?'

'I'll tell you all about it later, I promise. Don't let's
think about it now.'

'All right. But it's genuine, isn't it?'

'Of course, perfectly genuine.'

'Well then, in that case . . .'

'That's right. Tell me: what are you going to do this
afternoon?'

'I suppose I shall have to go back to London, shan't I?'

'Do you mind if I come with you?'

'What's all this about?' She pulled at his arm until he
looked at her. 'What's going on? There's something else,
isn't there? What is it?'

'I've got to find somewhere to live.'

'Why? I thought you lived somewhere in this part of
the country.'

'Didn't Uncle Julius tell you about my new job?'

'For heaven's sake, tell me about this properly, Jim.
Don't keep me guessing.'

When he had explained, Christine said: 'I knew he had
some secret that was amusing him but I didn't know that
was it. It's perfect, isn't it? I say, there won't be any difficulty about your leaving your job with the University here,
will there?'

'No, I don't think so.'

'What job is it, by the way? The one he's given you?'

'The one Bertrand thought he was going to get.'

Christine began laughing noisily and blushing at the
same time. Dixon laughed too. He thought what a pity it
was that all the faces he made were intended to express

rage or hatred. Now that something had happened which really deserved a face, he'd none to fit the occasion. Then he noticed something ahead of them and slowed in his walk. 'What's the matter?' she asked.

'See that car?' It was Welch's, left slightly nearer one side of the road than the other, outside a teashop with green curtains and copper pots in the window. 'What's it doing there?'

'He's picking up Bertrand and the others, I suppose. Bertrand said he wasn't going to have lunch in the same house with me after what I'd said to him. Hurry up, Jim, before they come out.'

Just as they drew level with the shop-window, the door opened and a crowd of Welches came out and blocked the footpath. One of them was clearly the unmanly writing Michel, on stage at last just as the play was ending. He was a tall, pale young man with long pale hair falling from under a pale velvety cap. Aware that passers-by were approaching, the whole group, with the natural exception of Welch himself, began moving out of the way. Dixon pressed Christine's arm encouragingly and walked up to them. 'Excuse me,' he said in a fruity voice.

On Mrs Welch's face appeared an expression of imminent violent sickness; Dixon gave her a friendly bow. (He remembered something in a book about success making people humble, understanding and kind.) The scene was almost over when he saw that not only were Welch and Bertrand both present, but Welch's fishing-hat and Bertrand's beret were there too. But the beret was on Welch's head, the fishing-hat on Bertrand's as they stood motionless with wide-open eyes. Dixon drew in breath to denounce them both, then blew it all out again in a howl of laughter. His steps became uncertain; his body bent weakly. With

Christine dragging at his arm he stopped in the middle of the group, slowly folding up like a man with a stomach wound, his mouth open in an agony of laughter. 'You're . . .' he said. 'He's . . .'

The Welches moved away and began getting into their car. Moaning, Dixon allowed Christine to lead him away up the street. The high-pitched humming and beer-bottle noises of Welch's starter began behind them, growing fainter and fainter as they walked on until the sounds were altogether drowned by the other noises of the town and by their own voices.

GLOSSARY

(The abbreviations used are: n.=noun; v.=verb;
adj.=adjective; p.t.=past tense.)

A

ACCURATE: exact, without mistake; *accurate shelling*=firing big guns so that the shells land in the right place.

ADVANCE-GUARD: body of soldiers sent ahead of an army.

AFTER YOU: (polite expression) Please go first.

AGONY: extreme pain.

AISLE: passage between the seats in a hall.

ALERT: *adj.* watchful; ready for anything to happen.

ALLY: *n.* person who is on one's side; friend.

APE: monkey-like animal with no tail.

APPETITE: readiness to eat food.

APPRECIATE: to enjoy something good.

ARTY: (slang) having to do with the arts—used with disapproval.

AWE: wonder and respect.

B

BALL: an important (official) dance.

BALLET: an entertainment by highly trained dancers.

BAR: room where drinks are sold; long table at which drinks are served.

BARRIER: wall or fence; gate at the entrance to a railway platform; anything which keeps people apart.

BAY: *n. & v.* the sound of a large hunting dog.

BEAD: small coloured hard ball with a hole, worn with others on a string for ornament.

144

BECKON: to make a sign with the hand or fingers telling someone to approach.

BEER: a drink with a slightly bitter flavour made from grain.

BERET: a kind of cap worn in the north of France, now also worn by soldiers, artists, etc.

BISCUIT: flour mixture baked into a small dry flat shape.

BLACK EYE: a dark-coloured swelling round an eye as the result of a blow.

BLINDFOLD: with one's eyes covered (e.g. with cloth) so that one cannot see.

BLINK: to shut both eyes quickly (perhaps several times—as in a sudden bright light).

BLONDE: *adj.* very fair (of hair); *n.* woman with such hair.

BLOOD: *to be out for somebody's blood*=wish to punish or hurt somebody.

BLOUSE: a woman's garment like a shirt.

BLUSH: *n. & v.* going rather red in the face.

BORE: *v.* make someone tired through dullness; BOREDOM: being tired in this way.

BRACE: *v.* keep firm.

BRAKES: blocks or bands which can be tightened on the wheels to slow down or stop movement.

BRAY: *n.* the noise made by a donkey.

BREEZE: a pleasant light wind.

BRISK: quick and without much care.

BULLY: *n.* person who is cruel to those who are weaker than himself.

C

CARDIGAN: a short coat of knitted wool buttoned down the front.

CELEBRITY: a well-known person.

CHAT: *n. & v.* talking in a friendly way without a serious aim.

CHEMIST: man who prepares and sells medicines.

CHEW: to move the jaws to prepare food with the teeth for swallowing.

CHIN: the part of the face below the mouth (front of the lower jaw).

CHOKE: *v.* show the effects of having something caught in the throat.

CINEMA: moving pictures; the theatre in which such pictures are shown.

CIRCUS: an entertainment, usually in a very large tent, with performing animals, balancing acts, etc.

CLENCH: *to clench one's fist*=close the fingers to make the hand into a *fist* (see FIST).

CLOAKROOM: room in which one can leave coats and hats, wash one's hands, etc.

CLUTCH: *n.*—When the *clutch* of a car, usually moved with the foot, is engaged or 'let in', the engine is able to move the wheels.

COLLAPSE: *v.* lose strength suddenly and fall.

COMMON ROOM: a room in which members of the college teaching staff can meet each other.

COMPLIMENT: *n. & v.* saying (or doing) something to show one's good opinion of another.

CONDUCTOR: (on a bus) man who collects fares and looks after the passengers.

COUNTER-ATTACK: *n. & v.* meeting an attack with an attack.

CREAK: *n. & v.* making a noise like that of bending dry wooden boards.

CULTURE: the customs and ways of thinking which have developed in a people.

CUNNING: *adj. & n.* clever(ness) at deceiving.

D

DELIBERATE: *adj.* done on purpose; intentional after consideration.

DENOUNCE: to speak against (a person or thing) in public for wrongdoing; *n.* DENUNCIATION

DESERT: *v.* go away and leave.

DETECTOR: an instrument which shows the presence of something.

DINNER-JACKET: a short black coat worn for fairly formal evening occasions.

DISASTER: a sudden serious accident or misfortune.

DIZZY: *adj.* feeling as if one's brain were turning round (as after spinning quickly or looking down from a height).

DON: *n.* a university teacher; *adj.* DONNISH.

DRESSING-GOWN: long coat-like garment worn over night-clothes.

DRUNK: *adj.* & *n.* made foolish by strong drink; a DRUNK-ARD gets drunk frequently; DRUNKENNESS is the condition.

E

ELBOW: the joint in the middle of the arm.

ELOCUTION: the study of correct speech.

EMBARRASS: *v.* cause to feel awkward and uncomfortable in the mind; *n.* EMBARRASSMENT.

EXCHANGE: *n.* building where telephone lines are connected.

EXHIBITION: a public showing (of paintings, etc.).

F

FED UP: (slang) tired and angry with somebody or something.

FIST: a hand with the fingers closed as for striking a blow.

FLASK: a container which keeps hot liquids hot or cold liquids cold; a pocket container for strong drink.

FOCUS: the right distance to get a clear picture (e.g. with a camera); *out-of-focus*=not clear because the eye is not set to the right distance.

FOOTBALL POOL: competition in which large sums of money can be won by correctly guessing the results of certain football matches.

FRIVOLOUS: not being serious in one's behaviour.

FROWN: *n. & v.* lowering the eyebrows (as when angry or thinking hard—sometimes used as a warning).

FURY: sudden great anger; *adj.*, FURIOUS.

FUSS: *n. & v.* excited worrying; (slang) trouble.

G

GALLERY: upper floor at the back of a theatre or hall.

GENUINE: not false.

GESTURE: a movement of the hands as a sign; something done to show one's feelings.

GIN: a kind of strong drink (colourless).

GLAMOUR: magical excitement.

GRACIOUS: kind (usually to people of lower position).

GRANTED: *taking her for granted*=being sure that she was his when he wanted her, without his having to do anything to keep her love.

GRASS: *to keep off the grass*=not interfere with another's rights, especially where a girl is concerned (slang).

GRIN: *n. & v.* a wide smile.

GROPE: to move in the dark with hands out to feel one's way.

GROWL: *n. & v.* making a deep sound in the throat.

GRUDGE: *n.* a feeling of anger against a person because of something in the past.

H

HEARTY: openly and cheerfully friendly.

HERITAGE: *our common heritage*=that which has been given to all of us by those who lived before us.

HIGH HORSE: *to get on (to) one's high horse*=start behaving with great dignity and pride.

HOSTILE: of an enemy; like an enemy.

HUM: *n. & v.* making a sound as if singing with closed lips.

HYDROGEN BOMB: a machine for causing immense destruction in one explosion.

HYPOCRITE: a person who pretends to be good; HYPOCRISY: such pretence.

HYSTERICS: common name for HYSTERIA, an illness caused by nervous excitement resulting in loss of control; *adj.* HYSTERICAL.

I

IGNORE: to take no notice of.

ILLUSION: a deceiving appearance; belief in something which does not exist.

IMBECILE: *n. & adj.* weak-brained (person).

IMMINENT: likely to happen immediately.

IMPULSE: a sudden desire to do something.

INCENDIARY: a person who sets fire to buildings; INCENDIARISM: such acts.

INDIGNANT: angry at wrong done by another; *n.* INDIGNATION.

INDISPOSITION: illness (usually not serious or long-lasting).

INTERNAL: on the inside.

J

JACKET: a short coat.

JERK: *n. & v.* making a sudden quick movement; a single shake.

K

KNUCKLES: the outside of the joints between fingers and hand.

L

LAY-BY: place (extra width) by the side of the road where drivers can stop for a rest.

LECTURE: *n. & v.* speaking to a number of people in order to teach; LECTURER: one who gives a lecture; person employed to teach in a college.

LIFEBELT: a floating ring thrown into the sea to save a person in danger of drowning.

LIFT: *n.* a free ride (e.g. in somebody's car).
LIMP: *adj.* not stiff.
LORRY: a heavy goods-carrying motor.
LOUNGE: large sitting-room.

M

MARTYR: a person who suffers and dies for his beliefs; (more loosely) anybody who suffers.
MASK: a false face (masks were worn by the actors in the ancient Greek plays).
MEAN: *adj.* unfair or unkind in one's treatment of another.
MEDIEVAL: see MIDDLE AGES.
MERRIE ENGLAND—This reflects the idea that life in the Middle Ages (about A.D. 500 to 1500) was carefree and pleasant.
MIDDLE AGES: the period of English history from about A.D. 500 to 1500; *adj.* MEDIEVAL.
MILLIONAIRE: a man who owns more than £1,000,000.
MOAN: *n. & v.* making a low sound as if in great pain.
MOISTEN: to make damp.
MOTH: a winged insect which eats clothes (*Lepidoptera*).
MUFFLE: *v.* to put something over (the mouth) so that sound will not come out clearly.
MUMBLE: to speak without pronouncing the words clearly.
MUTTER: *n. & v.* speaking quietly without moving the lips.

N

NASTY: very unpleasant.
NATIONALIST: one who wants independence for his country.
NEDDY: children's name for a donkey.
NEUROTIC: having no control over the feelings.
NEUTRAL: neither on one side nor on the other.
NUDGE: *n. & v.* touching with the elbow (the middle joint of the arm).

O

OBVIOUS: clear; unmistakable.

OFFENSIVE: *adj.* rude and meant to hurt the feelings.

OLD BOY: a careless form of address to an equal, meant to sound friendly.

OPEN: *Open Week* = a week when members of the public are invited to see the work of a school or college.

P

PACIFIST: one who believes in peace at any cost and will not fight in time of war; PACIFISM: such beliefs.

PANG: sudden sharp pain.

PANIC: sudden unreasoning fear.

PANT: to breathe hard and quickly (as after violent exercise).

PARAGRAPH: a number of sentences grouped together; (in a newspaper) a short article.

PART-SONG: a song in which there are *parts* for various voices singing different notes at the same time.

PATRONAGE: the system by which in the past artists were supported for the public good by men of wealth (PATRONS).

PIANO: large stringed musical instrument (*pianoforte*) with keyboard.

PILL: a small solid ball of medicine; *sleeping-pills* = pills to help one to sleep (too many may be dangerous).

PILLAR: a stone (or brick, iron, etc.) support like a thick post.

PINCH: (slang) take dishonestly; steal.

PLASTIC: *n. & adj.* modern material used for making many things—it is shaped when hot.

POISE: calmness and confidence.

POOL: see FOOTBALL POOL.

POPSY: (slang) pretty girl; girl friend.

PORTER: a man who carries baggage; a college servant.

PRE-: before (e.g. *pre-lunch* = before lunch).

PRIG: a person who is conscious of his own goodness.

PROLONGED: continuing for a long time.

PROSTRATE: *adj*. lying flat.

PUB: (slang for *public house*) inn.

PUBLICITY: making something or somebody widely known.

PULSE: a place (e.g. at the wrist) where the blood can be felt beating; *to take someone's pulse*=find the speed of the heart-beats.

PYJAMAS: men's nightclothes; *adj*. PYJAMA.

R

RATTLE: *n*. & *v*. making a sound like that of many small hard objects knocking against one another.

REACTION: action which is the result, before thinking, of another action or situation; *v*. REACT.

REASSURE: to let someone know that there is no need to worry; *n*. REASSURANCE.

REBOUND: *v*. be thrown back (as a ball is thrown back when it hits a wall).

REMORSE: a feeling of sorrow for having done wrong.

RESEMBLE: to look like.

RIDICULOUS: so unusual as to make one laugh; very foolish.

RITUAL: a set of actions fixed by custom.

ROW: *n*. (slang) quarrel.

S

SACK: *n*. & *v*. (slang) dismissing from employment.

SANDWICH: *n*. meat or other flavouring between two thin slices of bread.

SARCASTIC: expressing scorn.

SCHOOLMARM: (slang word expressing disapproval) school mistress; *adj*. SCHOOLMARMY.

SCRIPT: written form of the actual words to be spoken.

SENIOR: *n*. & *adj*. older or more important (person).

SHERRY: golden-coloured strong wine from Spain.

SHILLING: in British currency before 1971, 20 shillings =£1

SHIN: the bone in front of the lower part of the leg.